Elle Klass
As Snow Falls

Word from the author

I'm often asked if this story is autobiographical. The answer is no. I wrote it during some of the darkest days of my life. It was the first novel I ever wrote. It was the first story longer than a couple pages I ever wrote.

Storm, as a character can be selfish at times but aren't, we all? She also learns to appreciate life and those she loves even when those lessons are hard learned.

As if rewarded she is given a wonderful life. Even that isn't always as perfect as it seems, and her journey doesn't end. It only leads to a new chapter.

Many people have asked if I'll ever write another story like As Snow Falls. The answer is no. It is a one of a kind just as our lives are one of a kind. We live, we learn, we love.

Enjoy the story.

As Snow Falls

Copyright © 2013 by Elle Klass
Republished 2020 Books by Elle, Inc.
ISBN: 978-1-951017-06-4
All rights reserved
Illustrations by Renae Van Brunt

Published by Books by Elle, Inc.
225 College Dr. #65504
Orange Park, FL 32065
www.elleklass.weebly.com

Author's Disclaimer:

Other Books by Elle Klass

Ruthless Storm Trilogy
Volume 1- Eye of the Storm Eilida's Tragedy
Volume 2- The Calm Before the Storm Evan's Sin
Volume 3 – In the Midst of the Storm Tommy's Deception

Evan's Girls
Book 1 – Scarlett
Book 2 - Emily

Baby Girl Series
Book 1- In the Beginning
Book 2- Moonlighting in Paris
Book 3- City by the Bay
Book 4- Bite the Big Apple
Book 5 – Caribbean Heat
Book 6 – Return to the Bay
Book 7 – Prison of the Past

The Bloodseekers
Book 1 – The Vampires Next Door
Book 2 – The Monster Upstairs
Book 3 – The Ghost Within

Zombie Girl
Book 1 – Premonition
Book 2 – Infection
Book 3 – Retribution

hidden journals
Volume 1 - Isandro

Prologue

As the snow falls gently upon the earth, leaving a patchwork quilt where bushes and dirt can still be seen, time stands still. No birds or animals can be heard, as they are snuggled away for the long winter ahead. Any sound would be heard for miles through the empty forest. The trees stand bare, and can be seen through as far as the eye can see. There is no wind blowing in any direction; just snow softly falling and covering more and more earth.

There lies a road still slightly visible, although no one has traveled it for some time. The road leads in one direction, up the mountain in a curvy path that resembles a corkscrew. This road with all its twists and bends travels over a now frozen river with low-water bridges. A few homes can be seen along this road with smoke emanating from their chimneys, leaving trails that climb into the cold, clear, snowing sky. A few lights can be seen through open drapes.

At the top of the mountain lies a small square log cabin.

The log cabin is surrounded by small bushes and trees that bloom with beautiful flowers in the spring and leave behind a fragrance of freshness and newness. Thirty feet behind the log cabin is a shed about ten feet by ten feet. Inside the shed are a work table, ride-on mower, and various pieces of yard equipment. On the west side, or front of the cabin, is a covered porch with two wooden rockers and a small round table. The cabin has five windows, two in the front, and one on every other side. The curtains are drawn in all but one, the largest window that faces the front. There is a front door; in fact, it is the cabin's only door, within a couple of feet of the cabin's largest window. Inside the cabin there are only two rooms.

The larger room is the main living space. To the south is a kitchenette fully equipped with a two-burner stove, a standard-sized refrigerator and freezer, and double sinks nestled directly below a small window with a Christmas cactus on the windowsill. A rug lies at the foot of the sink. A small countertop covers two lower cabinets. Above are two more cabinets. The walls are lined with shelves for plates, bowls, and glasses. On the stove there is a water pot now empty. Beside the sink on one of the countertops lays an empty dish drainer. In the middle of a small square wooden table with the sides folded down are fresh cut flowers in a clear vase. There are two wooden chairs placed on opposite sides of the table. The rug underneath is diagonal to the length of the table. In front of the table is a window that faces the west on the opposite side of the door from the largest window.

On the north side of the cabin there is a full-size bed with a quilt and two down pillows. Above the bed is another window. There is a tall bureau within two steps at the foot of the bed. On the bureau is a cell phone that appears to be turned off. There are also many pictures of a boy throughout his years. Some of these pictures are of him with a beautiful lady, a young boy, and a girl. The headboard touches the east wall of the cabin. Beside the headboard is a thick wooden oval cabinet with a TV on top. The TV is shut off.

Next to the wooden cabinet is the second room in the cabin, a bathroom. Inside there is a porcelain bath supported by four legs. From the ceiling, going all around the bath, is a shower curtain. In back of the tub is the final window in the cabin. To the south of the bathtub there is a commode with shelves above it holding shampoos, lotions, flower petals, and a small candle burning, leaving a scent of lilac. To the west of the commode is a sink with the only mirror in the cabin hanging above it. Three rugs sit in front of the tub, the commode, and the sink. The door of the bathroom faces west. On the east side of the wall, between the kitchenette and bath, is a small closet that contains cleaning supplies, extra towels, and sheets.

On the northwest corner of the cabin is a stone woodburning stove, burning brightly and feverishly, leaving behind a feeling of warmth and security. In the middle of the cabin is a large area rug covering most of the rest of the wooden floor. Two plush rocker recliners face the largest window to the west. Between the rocker recliners is a table with a lamp, a radio, and two empty coasters.

The snow continues to fall until the road is no longer visible and the lights in the houses have been turned off. The smoke from the chimneys continues to make its way out into the cold snowy night air. The only light now comes from the moon and the little log cabin at the top of the mountain. Inside the cabin an elderly woman sits, rocks, and watches the snow fall…

Sanctuary

Many years ago there was an image, a very faint image of darkness. Nothing could be seen—not even my hand—just blackness and a feeling. A feeling attached to the image and a sound, rhythmic and comforting. This was my home and it gave me a feeling of closeness, warmth, and sanctuary where nothing bad could ever exist, only goodness. Somehow God and everybody else had another plan for me that took me years to figure out. It seemed only cold harshness lay in front of me and on every side. The image remains clear in my head and the feeling in my heart. Suddenly there was a sound, a sound all too familiar to me. It was the sound of my warmth and sanctuary that said it was OK to come out. There was love, more love outside waiting for me, love I wouldn't know if I stayed where I was. I knew it was time. My sanctuary was over, and I had to

face whatever was beyond my dark, safe
walls.

As I emerged into the light, it was
brighter than I had ever before seen.
There were faint images or silhouettes of
things that made sound. Suddenly I was
placed into a warm, caring cradle where
I could hear and feel the pounding,
rhythmic beat that had soothed me in
my life so far. I felt almost at home, but
somehow lost in something I didn't
know that frightened me. The feeling of
sanctuary never went away, but it
became fainter over the years and
through my trials.

Over time the images and
silhouettes around me became bright
and vivid, full of color and detail. The
one called Daddy had chestnut-colored
wavy hair, always cut short, and green
eyes the color of the fuzzy stuff he
called grass that grew outside, but he
had soft stuff on his face that tickled
when he kissed me. The one called
Mommy had gold locks the color of the
world outside, and her eyes were also
the color of grass. She was the one who
held me most when I wanted to be held.

Daddy would always leave when the brightness came out and come back when the brightness started to go away. Sometimes he would stay all the time. It followed a pattern: five brightnesses, and he would stay home for two brightnesses.

Then there was the one they called my sister, or Emily. She had shoulder-length wavy chestnut hair and eyes the color of grass as well. She was the most interesting to me because she wasn't big. She was small like me, only a little bigger, and she would always be the first to come and make sounds at me every day. Sounds they called talking. I understood her sounds, and she understood mine. No one else seemed to understand mine, but they all seemed to understand hers, or at least they answered back with something that made sense to what she said. She would bring these things called books, sit down beside me, and talk about a book and its pictures, Mommy called this reading. Sometimes she would get on the ground and chase me around on all fours.

She could do many things
Mommy and Daddy could do like pour
herself a drink when she was thirsty,
turn on the thing that made noises
called radio, and she used only her legs
to get around. I wanted to do the same.
So far I could only move using my
whole body, including my arms and
legs. I wanted to do like her, so I
decided I needed to practice. I moved to
the large, soft, fuzzy thing they called a
couch, and I took my hands and slowly
lifted myself up. Now on my legs I was
taller, and I could see down. It seemed
like a long way down. Uh-oh, boom, I
fell. If I did it once, I knew I could do it
again. So I tried many, many times
before I was finally able to stand on my
legs, but once I could stand I made my
way through the room only to fall on
my hands and face. Somehow, once I
moved my legs, my body seemed to pull
forward until I was level with the
ground. I continued practicing this.
Mommy always said I was running.

My world seemed to grow
smaller. Emily now went to school. It
was just me, Mommy, and most of the

brightness, which I now know is called day. When Emily would come home my day would become alive again, but it seemed short lived, as soon it would be dark again. Seeing how lonely I had become, Daddy brought home a soft, furry creature he called a kitten, and he asked me and Emily to name it. Emily was the only person who seemed to understand me, so we decided to name it Mr. Fur. Mommy and Daddy laughed as they suggested Mrs. Fur, saying it was a *female kitten* but we wouldn't budge, and so Mr. Fur it was. Mr. Fur became my best friend as we played together and slept together for naps. She even lay beside me when I would fall asleep on the floor.

Many of the images have become fuzzy over time, but I remember clearly when Mommy said I needed to start using the thing called a toilet. It was huge and made noises when the lever was pushed down. It was so huge, in fact, I feared it would swallow me whole, and I refused to use it. This made Mommy very upset, but she didn't get mad. She was very persistent with my using it and wouldn't give up. She even bought me a small one of my own. This was much better, and it didn't have a lever that made horrible noises. It would be a long time before I faced the horror of the large toilet. Mommy took my small one away and said it was time for me to use the big one. I ran to my room and curled up on the floor with my blankets around me so she couldn't find me, and I could feel my sanctuary once again. It seemed like forever, but she never came looking for me. Under my covers I knew this was something I had to do like leaving my comforting sanctuary. If Mommy said it was all right I had to do it.

Slowly I lifted the covers and crawled out from under them. I listened at my door and couldn't hear anyone. I had to do this alone, face my fear by myself. With all the bravery I could get hold of, I slowly turned the knob and peeked out of my door into the hallway. I made my way into the hall and into the bathroom. Very carefully I scooted a little stool, which sat beside the sink, to the front of the toilet. Carefully I prepared myself and climbed up onto the giant toilet, which seemed to get bigger by the moment. I was very careful not to touch or lean back on the lever that made the loud noises. I did what Mommy wanted and quickly climbed off the toilet. In fact, I jumped off, put my clothes back on, touched the lever, and ran full speed ahead into Mommy. She laughed and asked what I was running from. It took awhile before I realized the lever that made loud noises wasn't going to hurt me but flushed everything away, leaving a clean bowl behind.

As long as I can remember, on the last day of the week, Sunday — Mommy and Daddy always said was the first day, but to me it was the last day of the week — we went to a place called church. In church they said and Mommy and Daddy agreed that somebody called God created the world, all the plants and trees, all the animals, and people. I couldn't imagine how somebody could do all that. They said he had a plan, a plan for every living creature, and nobody knew his plan, but he had one for all of us. In my small and still developing mind, I thought it was like me and my dolls. I brushed their hair, dressed them, and made them talk to each other. Did God somehow do the same thing? Were we his dolls? After church we would come home and listen to radio shows where there was always a good guy and a bad guy. The bad guy would always plan bad things to do to the good guys. Was that part of God's plan — that there is good and bad, the bad always trying to hurt the good? Was life about God and evil? They said the evil was something like God only the complete opposite. He came to take us away from God and make us his. Why would anybody want to be bad or evil? I wondered about these things for years and slowly the answers came, and as my mind developed, I understood more and more.

Sometimes on Saturdays we would go to a big place with many little places inside it called stores. There were always many people. The people all looked different. Some had short hair, and some had long hair and strange colors. Not all people had wavy and curly hair. Some people had hair that was straight, just like my clothes after Mommy would iron them. Most of the people had eyes the color of the sky or the color of Mommy and Daddy's coffee, which sometimes they would let me sip. Their skin was many different shades as well. Sometimes they spoke funny too, and I couldn't understand them. All these people were unique, and they all had something in common; they were all there to buy things or sell things.

In this place there was a special store that we always went to just before we left. In this store they sold food: hamburgers, hot dogs, pizza, and my favorite, ice cream. Mommy and Daddy always ordered me and Emily a plain cheese pizza and garlic sticks, made from the crust of the pizza. It is still the best pizza I have ever eaten. After our pizza, I would always eat a huge chocolate fudge sundae made out of chocolate ice cream with rich dark chocolate syrup, chocolate shavings sprinkled on top, and a slice of ice cream cone dipped in chocolate on the top. It took me awhile but I always ate my entire sundae, and then I went to sleep in the car all the way home.

Sometimes during the week, making sure Mommy was busy, Mr. Fur and I would sneak into Emily's room and play with all her pretty things. She had a large mirror above her dresser and many perfumes that smelled good and tickled my nose. She had stuff she put on her lips that made them shiny. My favorite was a box overlaid with fabric that had a beautiful ballerina in it that would spin and play music when opened. The ballerina had a satin bodysuit with a net tutu, and on pointed toes she would spin and spin. Inside the box were many pretty, shiny items that Emily would wear on her fingers, neck, and wrists. She called them jewelry, and she called the beautiful box a jewelry box. The shiny things that she wore on her fingers she called rings, the ones around her neck she called necklaces, and the ones around her wrists she called bracelets. Mr. Fur and I would put on her shiny lip stuff, pretty-smelling perfume, and all her jewelry, and we looked very glamorous. I don't think Mr. Fur agreed though because she would run under her bed, and I would have to force her out so I could put all Emily's beautiful things back so she wouldn't know I had been in her room. I am not sure why Mr. Fur didn't want to wear pretty things. Daddy buys Mommy pretty things all the time, like the sweet flowers we always had sitting in the middle of the table.

One day when we snuck into Emily's room, Mr. Fur got really mad and made me spill some of her perfume. The floor got all wet and stunk. I tried to clean it up and even sprayed the smelly stuff Mommy uses when she says the house stinks, but her floor was still wet and the smell was still there. Maybe it would be OK by the time Emily got home. I slowly closed her door and went back to my own room. When Emily got home, I kept her from her room by bringing her books to read, and we made a town out of building blocks, but eventually she had to go to her room. She came running out of her room crying, telling Mommy that I had spilled her perfume. Mommy went with her, and sure enough, they both came back and were very upset with me. I was sent to my room where I cried under my blankets in my sanctuary. I must have fallen asleep because when I woke up in the morning I was in my bed. When my daddy got home from work he brought me a jewelry box of my own, and when I opened it up there was a beautiful ballerina twirling. It played music as well, and inside it was a bottle of perfume and gorgeous jewelry for my fingers, neck, and wrists. Daddy said that I was big enough now to have my own.

The first time I remember meeting my grandparents was during Christmas. Emily and I had to share a room, and Grandma and Grandpa used mine. Grammy used our small spare room. It was just big enough for a bed and a dresser. Grandma was always praying. She would close the door to the room and pray. Mommy said not to disturb her, but I wanted to know what she was praying about all the time, so I slowly opened the door and snuck in beside her. She stopped praying and gave me some beads. They were pretty beads, and she had more. She had many beads, and they had different prayers that went with them. I knelt beside her and prayed with her, although I didn't really know why or what I was praying about. They were just prayers she had memorized that went with the beads, but I liked being there with my Grandma.

Grandpa listened to the radio, mostly sports. He would get mad at the radio sometimes, and he was always changing the stations back and forth. I am not sure how he listened that way, but I liked to sit with him. He would tickle my knees when I got too close and when I least expected it. Grammy was just fun. She liked to climb trees, go for walks, and once at the park, she went across the monkey bars and fell and hurt her wrist. We had to take her to the doctor, and they put a large fabric bandage around her wrist. They said it was sprained and that she shouldn't play on the monkey bars anymore. That didn't stop her though. We still had fun, and she would play my card games where I would always win.

Outside the snow continues to fall, and everything is covered in white. The only light comes from the little log cabin where the elderly lady with a slight smile on her face continues to rock. She watches the snow as it falls, covering the entire mountain as far as the eye can see…

The First Evil

So far in my life I had never seen evil. I knew bad; like when the bad guys in black hurt the good guys in white, and the toilet with the lever made loud frightening noises, or when I had snuck into Emily's room and spilled her smelly beautiful perfume all over the carpet, but I didn't have any concept of what evil was. All I knew was it was worse than bad; something so bad it couldn't be thought of. I was soon going to find out what evil was.

Mommy and Daddy said I was going to start school this fall. All I knew about school was what Emily had told me. She loved school, and she told me about reading and parties with lots of candy, cookies, cake, and all her friends. I had even met some of Emily's friends when they came over, and they were almost as interesting as Emily. Mommy bought me all kinds of new things like a box that opened to put my lunch in, new shoes, lots of new clothes, and my favorite — a bag for stuff. I could put many things in my bag; even Mr. Fur fit in my bag, and I liked to put her in my bag and run around the house. She liked it as well. I wanted to take her to school in my bag, but Mommy said my bag was for other stuff. Stuff like books, papers, pencils, and crayons. I don't know why anyone would want to waste such a good bag on those things, but when I wasn't at school I could put other things in my bag.

On the first day of school, Mommy drove me and Emily. The school seemed big. There was a huge building with doors that went into different rooms all around it, and there were two big doors that opened into a really big room with lots of tables. Emily said that was the cafeteria, and we would eat lunch in there. It must be something like a gigantic kitchen. I wondered if the stove and refrigerator were just as big. My classroom had five tables with four wooden chairs around each, and there were names on paper stuck to the tables. There were two windows and a big desk with a chair that seemed more comfortable than the wooden ones around the tables. The lady who Mommy said was my teacher was tall, had very dark large hair, and eyes the color of coffee. She also had wrinkles all over her face with creamy stuff gooped in them. She was scary, I thought, and to myself I called her the Boogie Woman. Mommy left, and I was alone with this scary woman and a bunch of children I had never seen before. I couldn't believe that Mommy would just leave me here, abandon me. I felt alone, and I just wanted to go home to Mr. Fur.

Boogie Woman was worse than I ever suspected, and so were most of the other children. There was a boy named Mark. He had long dark, stringy hair that covered his face. He always kind of stunk, and he usually wore the same clothes day after day. I could tell he was poor, unlike most of the other children. His family couldn't afford to buy all the neat clothes the rest of us wore. They must not have been able to afford much water either, because I don't think he took too many baths. All the other children made fun of him. They teased him about his shaggy-dog-looking hair and his tattered old clothes. Nobody ever said anything nice to him, and he had absolutely no friends. I always felt bad for him, and I wondered what it was like for him but I never talked to him, never said one word. I would always smile when he looked my way, but I didn't know what to say to him.

The kids were mean, cruel, and positively horrible, but they were nothing compared to Boogie Woman. She would get mad at him, because he couldn't read, and she would blame it on his shaggy hair saying, "Your hair is in the way, and you can't see the words on paper through it!" She may have had a point, because I don't think he could read through his hair, but I don't think he wanted to either. I don't think he wanted to be at school at all, and I didn't blame him, because I didn't want to be there either. School was a bad, bad place.

Life grew worse for Mark with each passing day. The kids would tease him by calling him names, poking at him, or throwing things at him, and the worst, they would take things from him like his lunch and run so he would chase them. Then they would throw it in the air, playing keep-away. Eventually they would throw whatever it was in the trash.

Boogie Woman would pin his hair back with bobby pins, and she'd tell him now he could read because his hair was out of the way. He still couldn't read. It didn't make a difference. When he got the chance, he would take out the bobby pins, or the other kids would, and then they would bend them and throw them at Boogie Woman. She would get mad and blame Mark. One day she got so upset with him because of his hair that she wrote his mom a note. Boogie Woman said that Mark's mom had to get his hair cut by tomorrow. Mark took the letter, and he didn't say one word. Next, she told Mark that if he didn't have his hair cut by tomorrow, she would put it up in pink barrettes. When Mark came to school the next day his hair still wasn't cut, and Boogie Woman put his hair back in bright pink plastic barrettes. She told him he couldn't take them out all day. He didn't take them out, and neither did the other kids, teasing him that he had bugs in his hair.

After a week of wearing barrettes at school, being teased every day, and beat up, he took them out in front of the teacher, broke them in pieces, and threw them away. That was the first aggressive thing Mark had done. He had never before tried to stand up for himself. Boogie Woman was furious, and she sent him to the office. After that day he got his hair cut, and he would leave the class during reading time. Slowly Mark learned to read. The next school year Mark would not take garbage from anybody and since he was bigger than they were, everybody became scared of him, and he was never teased again.

There were other children who were singled out and harassed. There was Maybell, who spoke with a lisp and had a hair lip; Timothy, who they called *Mongrel*, because his mother was black and his father was white; Francisca, because she spoke a different language and had one leg that was longer than the other; and Colt and Kim, who were twins and had no father. Their mother worked at the school. These children were teased and called *retards*, and nobody ever said a thing. The teachers turned their backs and walked away. I decided these children were smarter than the rest, and they would probably grow up to be powerful people if they made it that far in life without cracking first. Only the strong survive!

There were other teachers like Boogie Woman, and the kids picked on some of them. There was Mr. Wanks, who got upset with us whenever we said the word *I*; Ms. Smilt, who would yell at us in PE if we made a mistake; and Mr. Yickle, who looked like a cartoon character and taught us the same lesson every day. He also had really bad breath and stunk. There was Mrs. Findel, who always compared me to my older sister. She was a great student and I was only OK. Mr. Lymn was another teacher who got picked on. He was so fat that the kids would throw things at him just to watch them bounce off. There was also Mr. C—nobody could say his real name—he was very quiet, and he allowed the children do anything they wanted. Everybody wanted him for a teacher but those that had him had no respect for him, called him names, and stuck thumbtacks in his chair. It was no wonder that all I could think of in school was going home and what I would do when I got there. I would tell Emily about all the horrible things, but she said, *You worry too much about things you can't stop*, and that *I should worry more about myself and what school can teach me*. I loved Emily, and she was smarter than me, but she was wrong about this.

As my mind grew, so did my understanding of God, and I knew school was not right. It couldn't be right and good for children to make fun of children, children to make fun of teachers—and the worst—teachers that made fun of children, yelled at them, made them cry, and had no remorse for their actions. I had realized that school was the first evil in life. There was no other explanation for what occurred day after day. The devil had taken these people, and they had allowed him to make them evil.

Outside the snow was still falling, and the moon was bright. The elderly lady sat looking out the window at the snow — but really past the snow. She was looking at something, something else that only she could see.

Shape Shifters

I had seen evil take many forms at school, but I had been lucky enough to avoid it. I had two good friends, best friends, Sarah and Sammy, and I knew that even under the worst torture: broken kneecaps, starvation, or solitary confinement, I could always trust and count on them. We always stuck together and protected one another. School, the first evil, was full of many very bad things. One of the worst was the shape-shifters, as I called them. They had no real identity or place of their own. They melted into whatever form they needed to get them where they wanted to be. They had no remorse for their actions, or concern for those they might hurt. Shape-shifters didn't really have any friends, and yet they all pretended to be friends with each other. In fact, most people pretended to be friends with them. I think it was fear that caused people to want to be their "friend." They were afraid that they would make their lives horrible and talk about them if they didn't do what the shape-shifters wanted. They ran the school and the lives of everybody at school, even the teachers.

The shape-shifters were true evil. The head shape-shifter was Carry. She had very long strawberry-blond hair. Her eyes were the color of steel wool and just as coarse; they could scratch and scar the soul of anybody. Below Carry was Rebecca. Her hair was the color of night and her skin as pale as a ghost. Just looking at her, I believe, struck fear in everyone, as she looked like she just rose from the grave. Rebecca was Carry's ghoul; wherever one was seen the other was close by. They were the top tier of school society but beneath them was a small infrastructure of others. Jules, Regina, and Jennifer were next in line. They were drones, and they followed and did whatever Carry and Rebecca wanted. Most kids wanted to be this high up in school society. They all had classes together, and when one was absent they talked about her.

Each girl had a male counterpart. There was Marco. All the girls liked him, and they thought he was so good looking, but really he was just rich, or his parents were. His ghoul was Josh. Josh was head of every sport, stupid but athletic, or so he thought. Really, Josh was just chosen as captain of every sport, because nobody else was willing to fight him for the position. Beneath them were Matthias, Luke, and Lee. They did whatever it took to maintain their superiority as Marco and Josh's friends. This small group of kids was always seen together, whether they were at school or out on the weekend.

Most kids at my school had known each other since the first year, when it all began. The shape-shifters were the ones who made everyone's life horrible, at least everyone they didn't like. Because of that, Mark became the school bully, and countless other victims went over to his side. They were always on the defensive, countering any move made by the shape-shifters. The shape-shifters were always kind to new students. They acted sweet, showed them around the school, and asked them to hang out, but as soon as they found a reason to turn they did.

A girl named Annabel moved from another state. She spoke differently, with an accent. They immediately pulled her into their ranks, and they wouldn't allow others to get to know her. They mesmerized her with their false kindness, and they brainwashed her into thinking they were her friends. Really, they made fun of the way she talked, and they would speak like her and laugh. They talked about her parents and family as if they were pigs wallowing in a pile of dirt. Her family didn't have a lot of money, but they were very nice people. They went to my church, and I got to know Annabel. She was pretty, with eyes the color of cherrywood, and her complexion was like nobody's I had ever seen. It was a very light tan with a natural blush. The boys all liked her, because she was so beautiful. She was probably the most beautiful person I had ever seen. The female shape-shifters didn't like that. She was an instant hit, and she had gained more popularity than they had imagined. She didn't take a backseat to them or anyone.

With Annabel's rising stardom, the shape-shifters began spreading horrible rumors about her. They'd say she was so poor that her family lived in a motor home. They had no running water, so they had to wash their hair in toilet water. Since they couldn't afford toothpaste, they would spit in a cup and recycle it. Annabel was hurt, but nobody believed the rumors. This made Carry and Rebecca very angry. They became so angry they did the unthinkable. Something that was so horrible, Annabel would never recover. Carry and Rebecca had Jules, Regina, and Jennifer write Annabel's name and phone number in every public restroom in town with some type of nasty message attached to it. After this, Annabel left, and she never came back. Nobody ever knew what happened to her. She just disappeared.

After they scared Annabel out of town, everybody was scared, except me. I was mad—very, very mad. I decided that I would get these girls for what they had done. They just couldn't get away with treating people that way. I had my opportunity the next fall. A new boy named Tony came to town. Everybody knew that the shape-shifters had dibs before anybody else. He didn't know the infrastructure of our school society, and he liked me. He would go out of his way to talk to me. He wasn't very cute; actually, he was kind of a nerd, but he liked me, and this bothered the shape-shifters. They couldn't get close to him because Sarah and Sammy would always bombard them with questions, acting like they admired him.

He finally made his move. He asked me to be his girlfriend. Of course, I said yes. When Carry and Rebecca heard, they were flabbergasted. They acted like it was great that we were a couple, and they gave us their "blessing." I knew they were plotting, plotting against me. I didn't care. There was nothing, no matter how evil, they could do that would hurt me. I was an ordinary student with a lot of friends that couldn't stand the shape-shifters, including Mark. I had numbers on my side, while they only had fear. At first I felt satisfaction that we, the little people, had beaten the tyranny, but I soon realized I was playing with a person's feelings. Tony really thought I liked him. He had a great personality, was very funny, and we started to become friends. I felt weird being his girlfriend, because I didn't like him that way. I finally confronted him, and I told him I really didn't want to be his girlfriend anymore, but I still wanted to hang out with him as a friend. He seemed happy and relieved. We stayed friends, and the shape-shifters never got their claws into him. I felt as though I had rescued him from something awful.

The snow outside was now so thick, no car could make it to the top of the mountain. The snow just continued to fall silently and cover everything in its path. The elderly lady just sat and rocked quietly. The only sound that could be heard in the cabin was the sound of her chair creaking on the wood floor.

The Second Evil

I had now seen evil take many forms, and I felt quite confident in foreseeing it and avoiding it before it could envelop me. I had seen many others get stopped in its path. It was like a wicked F5 tornado that destroyed anything that got in its way. I was not prepared though for what evil was about to encompass me.

At home, Emily was leaving. She had received a scholarship for a prestigious university. It was now just me and Mr. Fur, all alone. I snuggled in bed with Mr. Fur, and I wondered what life would be like now. Daddy left with Emily on a Saturday to drive her to school. Mommy and I walked Daddy and Emily outside. It was hot already, and the sun was starting to peek out. The car was packed with all her things. Mommy gave her a kiss, and I gave her a hug, and we wished them a safe trip. We watched until we could no longer see the car. Mommy went inside, but I stayed outside and stared. I stared until my vision was a blur. There really were no thoughts in my mind, just loneliness. As I went back into the house I stopped in Emily's room. It was so empty. Her furniture was still intact, but there were no clothes in her closet, no items on her dresser, and most of all, no Emily to liven up the room. I remembered all the times I played with her makeup and wore her jewelry when she was at school, all the times she would read me books and give me advice about the world—the evil, wicked, horrible, cold, cold world. I would have to rely on myself and my own instincts now. I lay down in her bed with Mr. Fur, and I went to sleep.

I must have slept in Emily's bed all day, because when I woke up it was dark. I could hear Mommy in the living room, but I didn't hear Daddy. What time was it? Why wasn't he home yet? I nervously scrambled out of bed. I had a feeling in the pit of my stomach. The feeling wouldn't go away. The more awake I became the stronger the feeling. As I reached the living room, I could see Mommy on the couch, glued to the TV.

That was unlike her. She never really watched TV by herself. Something bad happened, something I knew I would never forget. It would haunt me for the rest of my life.

I went to the couch and could see Mommy crying in her hands. On the TV were reporters. What were they saying? It sounded like jumble; my mind wouldn't process what they were saying. I pulled myself together, and I looked at the pictures. The pictures were showing buildings, some huge skyscrapers knocked down. They looked as if a huge bulldozer had come along and run over the tops of them. A bridge had collapsed and many people had fallen into the river. I was finally able to hear what they were saying. There had been a massive earthquake, maybe the largest North America has seen yet. I was mesmerized by the news; what did it mean? I stared at the TV unable to speak, unable to think. Finally, I asked Mommy where Daddy was. She looked at me with tears in her eyes, and she held me. We sat that way for what felt like forever. Then she looked at me and said, "I don't know." We stayed glued to the TV all night. Mommy eventually fell asleep curled up on the arm of the couch. I couldn't sleep. All I could do was think, *Are my Daddy and Emily out there somewhere?* There were rescue crews digging people out of buildings and cars. None of the cars looked like ours.

With nothing more that I could do I had to help Mommy. I went into the kitchen and fixed some coffee, scrambled eggs, and waffles. She woke up from the smell. We sat and ate as much as we could. Although neither of us was very hungry, it seemed like the thing to do. We kept ourselves busy all day, cleaning. We must have cleaned every nook in our house, places that had never been cleaned before. That night we both slept in my parents' bed. I hadn't done that for years, but at the moment I didn't care how old I was. I didn't know if my sister or dad were all right, and I was scared. I woke up to a soft caress on my cheek. It was Daddy. He was home and alive. I hugged him. I hugged him so hard he told me that I squeezed the stuffing out of him.

The next day he told me and Mommy all about everything. Emily was fine. She was at school. He was on his way back when the earthquake happened. He backtracked to Emily's school, but no damage was done. The phones were out because of the earthquake. He then headed back home, but with so many of the roads closed, he spent most of the time in the car trying to get home to us. He said he had never seen such disaster or devastation in all his life. When the earthquake happened he was in the car, and he said the concrete road moved in waves before his eyes. I was just glad to see him home, and I was glad to know that both he and Emily were alive.

After the earthquake, I changed. It changed me and everyone around me. Many of my friends and classmates at school had lost loved ones and friends. I was lucky. Battles and problems that existed before the earthquake now seemed infantile and didn't matter. We grew closer, and we helped each other.

People in the community stepped forward to give blood, donate food, and some families even opened their homes to people who had lost theirs, like our neighbors across the street. I was amazed that something so devastating could bring the good out in people.

My parents invited our neighbors and their new housemates over for dinner, and that is when it happened. That night I met Cobie. Cobie had a smile, kind of half a smile with a dimple on the right side of his mouth. He had blue eyes the color of the oceans from space. I couldn't say anything all night. I was captivated. All I could think about was Cobie. He was in every thought in my mind. I wondered what he was like, and how I could get to know him. I urged my parents to invite them over again to watch TV and have ice cream. Finally they relented, and they asked them over. We watched TV, and I took orders for ice-cream sundaes. To my amazement, Cobie asked if I needed help. I almost couldn't speak, but I squeaked out a yes.

We had fun making sundaes, and afterward we had an ice-cream topping fight in the kitchen. I don't know what spurred me to do it, but I started the fight by throwing sprinkles in his hair. He then smeared chocolate all over my face, and it was on. We had covered each other in nuts, chocolate, sprinkles, and caramel, and it was all over the floor as well. We couldn't help but laugh at each other. After we cleaned up the kitchen, we sat on the back porch looking at the stars. He pointed out all the constellations to me. He seemed to know everything about the nighttime sky. He had unlocked the mysteries that it held. Cobie seemed so real, unlike many of the kids I knew who hid their real selves behind a façade. It was definitely one of the best nights of my life, and I never forgot it.

I continued to try to get Cobie's attention, and from time to time I would. I knew he felt the same way about me that I felt about him, but he was so shy that he never seemed to get up the nerve to ask me out. I didn't know what to expect from him. One minute we would be laughing and teasing each other, and the next we would be upset at one another because one of us had gone too far. There was always a distance and curiosity in our relationship that sent mixed cues. I would go out of my way to catch a glimpse of him.

His father bought a garage in town. Cobie worked there after school most days. Sarah, Sammy, and I would go for walks, and I would purposely make them walk by the shop with me. He was always too busy working on a car to notice me. How was an engine better than me? His parents bought a house in town just few blocks from my house. I would go to the store for my mom, and I'd purposely take a longer route so I could walk by his house. One afternoon he was there. He was in the driveway, and as usual he was messing with a vehicle. It was an old faded red truck. I went up and said hi to him, and we talked for a few minutes. I asked about his truck, and I found out it had been his grandfather's truck.

I asked to see his house, and he showed me around inside very quickly. Then I caught sight of a tire swing outside in the backyard. He took me into the backyard, and I jumped on the swing. He jumped on with me and we twisted and twirled until we both fell off laughing, with our heads spinning. After a few minutes he stood up, grabbed my hand, and pulled me up. Next, he grabbed my other hand, walked me up against the tree, raised our hands above our heads, and he kissed me, openmouthed. It was an incredible feeling and I found myself kissing him back. My body felt like it was being lifted off the ground. Then reality hit me on the head like a brick, and I dropped back down to earth. What was I doing kissing this boy I didn't really know? What kind of a person did he think I was?

I slipped out from under his grasp, and I went running through his house and most of the way home. I couldn't help myself, and I kept thinking about that kiss. I had never been kissed like that before by anybody.

I couldn't help thinking about the kiss, and against what I knew was my better judgment, I wanted it to happen again. I felt guilty for kissing him and wanting him. At school I had always gone the long way to get to my classes, so I could pass by him. It had given me a reason to say something to him or to catch a glance; to meet his eyes with my own. Now I didn't go the long route anymore. One evening he came by my house, but he didn't come in. He parked, stepped out of his truck, and headed for my house. Then he suddenly stopped, went back to his truck, got back in, and sat for a few minutes. Then he drove away. I continued to hold out for him, but there were so many mixed messages. I wasn't sure what he wanted. There were many guys at school asking me out, so I finally relented and went out with one of them, Nathan.

Nathan had hair the color of coal and eyes the color of coffee beans. He had an older brother — who was much older and no longer lived at home — and a twin sister. He was very outgoing, the opposite of Cobie. He lifted weights and wrestled. I always went to his wrestling matches, and I cheered him on. I had become involved in acting through school and the community theater. Nathan always supported me; he came to watch my plays, and he helped me practice my lines. He planned on joining the military when he graduated, and he wanted me to follow my acting career. He said I was a natural, and acting was a dramatic outlet for me.

My father had nicknamed me Storm when I was just a baby. Nathan said Storm was the perfect name for me, because I was unpredictable and high strung. Nathan was always strong, courageous, and sure of himself. We were opposites. I never felt sure of anything, but being with Nathan I felt strong and decisive. We became very close and spent the next couple of years together. My parents loved him, and he spent a lot of time at our house.

We did practically everything together, and I enjoyed being with him, but I was never able to get Cobie out of my mind. That night we spent together looking at the stars—and the incredible kiss — were etched in my brain forever. I would look out my bedroom window on clear nights and find the constellations. With each constellation I found I could picture Cobie's face with his crooked smile and dimple. I could even smell him. It was as though I drifted back into time if only in my mind.

At school we had one big event that we all looked forward to but only few would attend: the senior prom. Nathan was a senior, and he asked me to the prom, Cobie was a senior as well, but he was going with his overpowering little girlfriend. She was small, loud, and she dragged him around like a puppy. I really don't think she was his girlfriend, since he had never really had one, but he was there with this girl. I couldn't stand it. I didn't know why he allowed himself to be treated that way. I would have never treated him like that, but he had made his choice, and I had made mine. The prom was beautiful; it took place in a hotel ballroom. Everyone looked beautiful, and I felt on top of the world to be there. Nathan and I danced most of the night. Afterward, Nathan, I, and our friends went to breakfast at an all-night coffee shop, and then he took me home. It was a wonderful night. After I got inside the house, I couldn't sleep. I felt like I was still dancing. As I lay in my bed I suddenly got another horrible feeling, but I couldn't place it. Everything in my life was perfect. I sat on the edge of my bed, and I looked out into the morning sky as the sun was coming up. I couldn't help thinking of Cobie.

The next afternoon, Nathan came by with big news. He was both excited and nervous. He seemed scared, and Nathan doesn't get scared. He is strong and sure of himself, but at the moment something seemed both wrong and right. His big news made my belly drop. It dropped into the pit of my stomach. I felt like my legs and arms were made of jelly, but somehow I knew it was good. There was a reason he had chosen to make this decision. He always thought a lot about everything, and he had mentioned this option to me before. I always supported him, but I never

really thought this day would come. But
here it was. The day! He was joining the
military. He felt it was his duty like his
father's before him to support, serve,
and protect our country.

The day he left for the military
was an overcast, rainy day. The sun
could not be seen, and I knew in my
heart that he was the one. As much as I
liked Cobie and still thought of him, I
knew that Nathan was the one. He
would make a good husband and father
one day. I went with his family to the
train station and watched his train
depart until I couldn't see it anymore.
On the ride home I was very quiet. I
listened to his father talk about how
proud he was of him, that he was
making the right decision, and — like
him — Nathan would have a good career
in the military. After I got home I went
to the back porch and stared at the stars.
Only this time, I didn't think of Cobie. I
thought of Nathan. He was so far away,
and until this day I hadn't realized I was
in love with him. I had always hung on
to Cobie, but he wasn't the one; Nathan
was.

The next year was lonely. I spent a lot of time with Sammy and Sarah. We would go to the movies together, or we'd go to each other's houses and stay up all night watching scary movies and eating popcorn. It was fun but didn't fill my void. I even got a part-time job, and I learned to drive. I saved up my money, and I decided to work on my grades so I could get a scholarship like Emily. Emily was now in law school, working on a degree. I knew I wasn't that smart, but I wanted to go to school and have a career. Mostly, I think it gave me something to focus on.

Nathan called when he had the opportunity, and he always sent me letters. For my birthday he had a dozen roses and a box of candy delivered to my house. The roses I dried and placed in one of my letters from Nathan. Somehow I made it through the year, but the worst was yet to come.

Nathan wrote me and said he was going to war. I always feared that, and my stomach started acting up again. I kept telling myself to be strong and stay busy. I no longer received regular correspondence from Nathan, but occasionally a letter would make it to me. I wrote him a letter almost daily, but I don't know how many actually made it to him. He said I gave him strength. I was glad I gave someone strength, because I didn't have any. Every day felt like the last, and I was in a dark tunnel trying to reach the light, but it kept slipping away from me. Finally, I decided to send out letters to colleges to see if any would accept me. I had decided to follow acting, and I chose colleges that had the best performing arts programs. My parents supported my acting, but they also said I should choose and work on another profession so I had backup while I tried to make it as an actress. After a few months, I started to get correspondence from the colleges, and I was accepted by one of them. I went off to college the next fall.

The summer before I left for college has stayed with me always. It was a very hot, slimy day. I finally received a letter from Nathan. It had been months, and I had even wondered if he was alive, but I kept praying. I knew somehow he would make it back. I was so excited I ripped into the letter. He wrote to let me know he was coming home soon. I was ecstatic until I looked at the date on the letter. This letter was months old. Why had it taken this long for it to get to me? Worse, where was Nathan? If he was coming home, how come he wasn't here?

No sooner had I read the letter then someone pulled up in the driveway. I ran outside to see who it was. It wasn't Nathan but close; it was his father. Uh oh, there was only one reason he would be here to see me, and I knew it wasn't good. I felt the same way I had when I didn't know what happened to my father. I got lucky that time; would I be lucky now? As his father came closer to me, I felt like I was going to drop. The bright light in the tunnel that was starting to peek out at me just got so far away that I was in pitch blackness. The next thing I knew, I woke up on my couch. I had a rag on my forehead, and I could hear my parents talking with Nathan's father. I just lay there knowing I didn't want to know why he was here, so I pretended I hadn't awakened. My mother came over to check on me, and now knew I was faking. She quietly talked to me, and I sat up. She told me that I had fainted, and that everything would be OK. Nathan's father came by to let us know that he was coming home. Unfortunately, he had been injured in the war, but it wasn't life threatening. He had lost part of his arm. I waited and waited for Nathan to come home, but he never did. That, in fact, was the last letter I ever received from him.

Life is full of ups and downs. I felt like I was riding on the earthquake that devastated me, but it brought me to Cobie. Cobie was a person I hadn't thought about in a while, and I didn't want to think about him now. I didn't know what happened to Nathan, but I was angry; I thought he couldn't face me. I loved him no matter what, even if he lost part of his arm. All that had mattered at the time was that he was alive. I became very hurt and angry, and I decided love had to be the second evil.

I thought love truly didn't exist; it was only for a few lucky people. I had somehow been weakened by Emily's going to college and the earthquake to allow myself to fall in love. It would never, ever, ever happen again. I became very cynical, and I swore to never again give in to the second evil, love.

The snow finally stopped falling, but it was so thick not even an emergency vehicle could have made it to the top of the mountain. The elderly lady just kept rocking in her chair, watching the snow, while a tear slowly rolled down her cheek.

A New Beginning

Now in college, I had decided I was free. College was such a wonderful place. There was always some event going on—concerts, football games, and parties. It was incredible. I was completely free to date anybody I wanted, and free to do as I wanted. I had decided I wanted to stay in college forever. Why would people ever leave such a place? Why choose a profession and go to work when you could stay here and do nothing but everything. Since losing Nathan, I no longer felt like acting. That part of me had died when he left. He had been my strength and rock, and with him at my side I knew I could be a star. Now I just wanted to be young and carefree.

My parents wanted me to take life seriously and choose a career; the school made me choose a major. Really, I had no career or life aspirations anymore. The major I chose was math, because I was good with numbers and could calculate without thinking. Really, math seemed like a boring career, but this major didn't force me to think hard, and I could enjoy all the benefits the college life offered. There were a lot of good-looking guys, and I would date a different one each Saturday. But I never went out with the same one twice. Going out twice might give them a false sense of security. They'd think I really liked them and wanted a relationship, which I didn't—just dinner, movies, and dancing.

The college I attended was a large performing arts school located downtown. It really wasn't just a performing arts school anymore, and they continued to grow and bring in new degree programs. It was an older campus with one way in and one way out. It was located next to a river. The dorms were located toward the back by the river, and there was a walking path with benches along the river's edge. My dorm was same sex, and my room was large enough for three people. I started out with only one roommate, Tia. Like me she was a freshman. She was very shy, quiet, and had a tiny build. Her aspirations were to become a musician. She played the clarinet. I enjoyed listening to her play. She had such talent, and her music made me embrace the day. In the summer her music was like the sun cradling me in its golden arms. In the fall it was like the leaves changing colors, gently falling down to the earth, and resting. In the winter it seemed to echo through the empty trees, and in the spring it brought back life. It forced the trees to bud, the flowers to bloom, and me to venture outside to inhale spring's sweetness.

Sometimes her music would touch my soul and bring Nathan back into my life. If I closed my eyes I could feel Nathan beside me. I could smell his body and touch his hand as we walked along the river's edge. I would freeze these images in my mind. I didn't want them to go away, but somehow the harder I held on, the faster they would vanish. I'd find myself alone again with the enchanting sounds of her clarinet and tears softly rolling down my cheeks.

I just didn't understand why he didn't come back. Why had he left me?

My roommate had come from a small town where her boyfriend still lived. Sometimes he would visit, and he was so encouraging of her; he knew one day she would play in the symphony. Her mother had died when she was just a little girl. Several years later her dad remarried. She didn't seem too sure of her stepmother, a woman who was eight years younger than her father. She understood though how he needed companionship. She was the youngest of her five siblings, and she thought her dad couldn't face life alone now that she had left for college. I believe it was the pain in her life that gave her music such passion.

My second roommate moved in when we came back from our first Christmas break. Her name was Robyn. She was loud, and we really didn't like her at first. She wanted to be an actress, and she thought she had to be obnoxious and the center of everything. She acted as if the world belonged to and revolved around her. She always kept her makeup and hair perfect, and she dressed the part for each new day. Sometimes she would change her outfit three or four times a day, depending on the part she wanted to play. I didn't think she was much of an actress, just an annoyance.

The first summer we both stayed, and that is when we really got to know each other. She wasn't so bad, just in need of constant attention and self-esteem. That first summer she confided in me, and she told me about how she had been given up for adoption as a baby. The family that adopted her was wealthy and took good care of her, but she always felt some part of her life was missing. When she became twelve they told her about her adoption and what they knew about her biological parents. She wanted to meet her biological parents and get to know them. In her mind, she built them up and imagined they were wonderful people that just couldn't afford to have a baby. She had anticipated meeting them, and having them welcome her with open arms. She had envisioned that she was their beautiful love child.

When my roommate was fifteen, her parents had finally found her biological parents. They weren't married, nor had they ever been. Her adopted parents had gone out of their way to search for these people, but then they didn't want her to meet them. She insisted on meeting them, so they relented and went with her to meet her mother. Her mother was only willing to meet her one time. She didn't want to be a part of her life. My roommate had thought that somehow, when they met, she would change her mind; she didn't. She found out that her father had raped her mother, and she was the product. Her mother gave her up because she couldn't live with the daily reminder of this vile and degrading encounter. She never saw her mother again. Her father was in jail. He had not only raped her mother, but he had hurt others as well. He was locked up in jail for a very long time.

The first summer, my roommate Robyn and I found jobs at Smith and

Vyne's. It was a large retailer, and they sold everything from women's lingerie to bedding. I worked in the women's department that first summer. I did everything from working as a cashier to putting up new displays. I tended the fitting rooms, put away clothes, and straightened the racks. Everything had to be in its spot and perfect. Their goal was that everything be attractive, color coordinated, and sized to make it appealing to the customer. My manager would walk around, look for items out of place, and make lists of incredibly ridiculous time-consuming tasks for us to complete. The days she wasn't there were much better. We would talk and help customers make important decisions about their clothing purchases. My manager always wanted us to tell the customers that any items they tried on looked good, but when she wasn't there we were more honest and made better sales.

My roommate worked in the bedding department. We worked crazy hours, but we were able to keep our schedules similar. Neither of us wanted to walk home alone at night, so when we worked nights we worked them together. The store was attached to the mall, and we would take our lunches together and eat at The Carousel. It was a high-notch restaurant for a mall. They loved her there, and they always seemed to have a table for us. Her parents had given her a credit card for school, and we usually ate at their expense. Occasionally though I insisted that she allow me to pay. The food was great. It amazed me how they could make something as simple as a hamburger and turn it into a chopped steak. Their French fries were even gourmet potato wedges slightly seasoned. She usually ordered a salad, as she always was concerned about her appearance and her weight. I didn't care, so I ate whatever it was my stomach growled for. The following two summers we continued to work at Smith and Vyne's, and I must have worked in every department the store had from women's clothing to men's clothing and jewelry.

Just like school at home, there were shape-shifters. They lived in sorority and fraternity houses, and they were the wildest partiers of all. They weren't like in grammar school, and nobody was really mean to anybody — unless they were going through initiation. There were some cruel things that went on, but usually nobody was hurt, just embarrassed when it was over with. It wasn't uncommon during pledge week to see guys running around in dresses and high heels, or for them to be absent from classes because of the inedible concoctions they ate or their massive hangovers from chugging contests. The sorority houses had a slightly different take on pledge week; the girls were involved in scavenger hunts and strange rituals such as being locked in a candlelit room wearing nothing but robes and performing a séance-like ceremony.

I decided I could party and have fun without formally belonging to a group and embarrassing myself in front of the entire student body or being scared out of my mind. My friends and I would go out every Friday. We met at Frank's Pizza House. It was the cheesiest, greasiest, sloppiest, and best pizza around. After pizza we headed for the movies and watched whatever was playing. Life here was great!

I always went home for Christmas and holidays, but I stayed and worked over the summer. The first Christmas was the worst. When I left for college I left everyone behind, including Sarah, Sammy, and Tony. I hadn't said a word since. In my solemn, depressive mood I cut everyone off, ran away, and was quite pleased with my decision. I really didn't want to go back home. I was happy, and going home would just remind me of all the reasons I left — of all the sadness that devastated my life there. I didn't want to know any more about Nathan, and I was afraid his dad would show up with more bad news. I had wiped the slate clean and started all over again, a new beginning. There was nothing there for me but my parents and to see Emily. She had been so busy that we hadn't seen her much after she left for college. We saw even less of her when she entered law school.

I had released my old self, and it went so far away I thought I would never find it again. But once in my parents' house, everything came flooding back. My old self came and rested beside me. It dictated my actions, thoughts, and well-being. I hid in my parents' house all Christmas vacation. I didn't come out. I didn't want anyone to know I was there. At night I lay in my bed with my blanket snuggled around me for security and Mr. Fur at my feet. It was my sanctuary and offered me peace and solace. The world would disappear, and I would fall into a deep sleep that led to dreams of happiness. The world before I knew what evil was.

The restful dead and long-forgotten would visit my sleep. My grandmother and I would pray using her incantations with beads for every prayer. Grammy was there swinging with me and descending down huge twisting slides. Grandpa was there watching sports and tickling my knees just like he did when I was a little girl. Sometimes I was a little girl again. We would all go for walks together and enjoy the fresh air. I would sometimes be at the mall with my family eating huge sundaes and falling asleep during the ride home.

Once I was with Nathan again, and everything was perfect; we were laughing and playing hide-and-seek. We were on a snow-covered mountain hiding behind ancient trees and snowy barriers. I hid in a huge dead tree with an opening in the bottom large enough for me to squeeze into. I heard him in the woods looking for me and calling for me. Finally he found me, but it wasn't Nathan anymore. It was Cobie. I ran out, found a mammoth drift of snow, and rolled the largest snowball ever. I threw it at him, and soon a snowball came hurling my way. It was on, the most vicious snowball fight ever. After the snowball fight we found ourselves snuggled in a cabin with a warm, glowing fire in front of us. I wasn't sure what these dreams meant, but I didn't care because they helped me keep my sanity during this very trying visit home.

The night before I left to go back
to school I couldn't sleep and found
myself staring out the window,
counting the stars in the sky. It was a
perfectly clear night. Every star could be
seen, and the moon was bright and full.
The air was dry with a chill in it. There
were so many stars in the sky that I quit
counting after I reached ninety-six. I
started to confuse myself, and thought it
better to stop. Instead, I found all the
constellations. The Little Dipper and Big
Dipper were always the easiest to find.
It was funny how all the stars formed
pictures and images that resembled
people and objects. They were all in
clusters, but I knew if I were in space
with them they would all seem so far
away from each other. Looking out my
window they appeared to be close
neighbors. They would blink and
twinkle at each other as if it were some
secret message they would send
throughout the universe to
communicate. I must have sat by the
window staring out for hours,
mesmerized by the magic in the sky.
Suddenly the stars seemed to rearrange

themselves, attempting to give me an intergalactic message. The message appeared to be a face that materialized before my eyes. It was Cobie's face. I fell asleep staring out the window at the stars.

The sky was clearing and the stars were beginning to peek out from the clouds. The elderly lady appeared to have shifted her gaze from the snow to the sky as she sat and rocked. The light of the stars made something twinkle around her neck.

The Third Evil

The next two years at college went pretty much like the first two. I started to lose interest and became bored. College had seemed so wonderful at first. It was an escape from my life, from everything that was ailing me, and I needed that escape to be able to move forward. I felt ready now to move on, and graduation was a welcomed event. My parents were there and so was Emily, who was now a prosecuting attorney. She seemed to love her work even though she hadn't been doing it for long. She was also engaged, and they set their wedding date for the following April. He was also an attorney, but unlike her, he was a business attorney and worked for a large corporation. They appeared to be made for each other.

Graduation itself was a boring, dry event. Speakers came up and gave long, subdued, sleepy messages about our lives ahead of us. How we were just now embarking on the great journey life has for us. How we needed to grab hold of our futures; the sky is the limit. I wanted to puke, but I was able to keep it down. After the ceremony I went to dinner with my family, my friends, and their families. We all celebrated the event together. Emily and her fiancé went back home the next day. As attorneys, they didn't seem to have much spare time. Maybe that was the secret to their relationship. They spent so little time together that the moments they had counted for double.

My parents stayed for an extra day, and they helped me pack. I received a job offer in an accounting firm, and I started work in just one week. That didn't give me much time to pack and move, so my parents helped out. I had found an apartment with a roommate I didn't know, but I hadn't known my college roommates either at first; it hadn't taken us long to hit it off and become friends though. I hoped the same would happen. It was the beginning of a new chapter in my life that forever changed me.

My apartment was in an old brick apartment building. There were oleanders around the front with beautiful white and pink blooms. Inside the apartment building there was a narrow staircase that went up three flights with a landing between each level. My apartment was on the second floor. The doors seemed narrow and smaller than usual, but it was very charming. My roommate had left the door key above the door, as she had said, and we entered the apartment. It was small. There was a miniature hallway that turned and led to the main room. The main room was a living area with a tiny kitchenette. There was another miniature hallway that led to the two bedrooms and one bathroom. The bedrooms were narrow and looked like huge closets. The bathroom was large, and it had a pedestal sink, a bathtub, and a shower with a curtain that went all the way around. There was a large linen closet before entering the bathroom. The apartment was sparsely furnished, and the walls were covered with flowered wallpaper. There were no pictures on the walls, but there were windows in every room, and it appeared as though the whole city could be seen from them. The apartment was located only a couple of blocks from where I would be working. We quickly brought in my few boxes and started unpacking. I didn't have much, but I didn't need much either. After we finished unpacking, my parents left so they could catch their train back home.

My roommate came home about six. She was approximately five feet tall with a soft pudgy build. Her eyes were warm and inviting. She was extremely friendly and outgoing. Most of the conversation was dominated by her. She took me out and around the neighborhood, filling me in on all our neighbors. Underneath us lived an elderly couple who had difficulty getting around, but every morning like clockwork they would go for a short walk to get fresh air. She loved to bake and the smells would permeate the walls of the building, making it an inviting place to be. He loved to fix electronic things. He would do this for everybody in the neighborhood. He would never accept monetary payment for it, although people paid him in other ways. The neighbors across the hall from them were young, and they had a little girl. Across the hall from us was a really strange young man. He was very quiet, and he came and went mostly at night. Nobody really knew anything about him; I guess that's what made him seem weird. Our neighbor above was an older man who had inherited the building from his parents. It was the house he grew up in. When the area turned into a business district he decided to cash in, and he turned the house into apartments.

We stopped in a charming diner for dinner. It was narrow with windows across the face of it. Inside it had a row of barstools around the kitchen area and a row of tables in front of the windows. It smelled of coffee and home-cooked goodness. What was wonderful about the diner was that it served breakfast, lunch, and dinner all day long. The staff was friendly. The food was OK, but I don't imagine people came for the food.

It was the ambiance, the charm, and they were open twenty-four hours a day. We sat and talked for hours, and filled up on coffee. She told me all about her job. She worked as a public relations representative for a local, up-and-coming firm. She loved her work, and I imagine with her bubbly personality she was perfect for the job. I told her what I knew about my job, which wasn't much. I would be working for an accounting firm, crunching numbers all day. We finally walked back to the apartment. It had been a very long day, and I was ready for bed.

The following Monday I started my first job. At first I loved it because I had financial freedom and got to dress up. I learned to wear flats though, as I walked to work every day. At lunch most of us in the office went together. It seemed exciting the first month or so, but soon the excitement started to wear off. I seemed to do the same boring thing every day. The boring monotonous pattern followed my life. I woke up, went to work, came home, and went to bed. Sometimes on the weekends I would go out with my roommate or one of my coworkers. My roommate had a boyfriend. He was the complete opposite of her—very subdued, tall, and thin as a pole. I wasn't sure how they tolerated each other, but it seemed to work for them. She always tried to fix me up with people, and we would go out as couples. I really wasn't interested. I had dated so much in college I didn't want to date now, and I certainly didn't want to meet anybody. I was happier continuing my repetitive routine and sulking in my own dismay of life. I continued to dredge on, but life seemed to be going in slow motion.

My roommate announced to me her impending marriage. They had already set a date. She talked with the owner, and he said I could keep the apartment. I didn't know if I wanted to though. I was really bored with my life, and I was ready for a change. She invited me to the wedding, and the ceremony was beautiful—simple but beautiful. The reception after the ceremony was full of life. It was the most exciting and interesting event I had encountered since leaving college. Her family was a lot like her. They were gregarious and loud, but always laughing with smiles on their faces. We ate, danced, and mingled. It was great! I almost envied her, because she had found happiness in such a vile, repulsive world.

I stayed in the apartment for a couple of more months. I managed the rent on my own, but I was more bored than ever. I didn't even have a roommate to keep me company. I received a letter from one of my college roommates; she had received a job acting in a soap opera. It was a small temporary part, but she wanted to make her character a regular character. I took a day off work just to watch her perform. Soap opera acting seemed to become her, as she lived her life like a soap opera. I didn't go out much anymore and saved my money. I wasn't sure why, but I was obsessed with saving money — maybe because I had nothing else to keep me grounded.

My work was going nowhere. I looked at numbers all day long. The numbers would take on a life of their own, dancing around the pages and swapping places like a game of musical chairs. It was hard to focus on them, and my eyes would hurt. I thought if I didn't leave this job soon I would end up wearing soda bottle glasses. My head would pound, and it felt like it was going to explode, coating the walls with my brain matter.

My boss was tall, thin as a pole, and always wore her hair back in a bun. She had thin skin and her veins could be seen. I could almost see the blood pulsing through them; when she became mad they seemed to throb. She was very shrewd and never smiled. Her lips were always in a straight line. The only way to tell when she was mad was to watch the veins in her face pulsating.

Work was a dismal, dark, and revolting place. I truly hated it, and I wanted so much to never go there again. It was so despicable and inhumane that I couldn't imagine why people had to be tormented this way. Were we so awful that we had to be punished daily for our iniquities by going to work with the only reward being pure survival? I had decided that work most definitely was the third evil in the world. The first was school, the second love, and now I had discovered work. Maybe it wasn't three evils at all, but a composite of a greater evil: the society in which we live. This society forces children to go to school and work, and it promotes love. Whatever it was, I couldn't do it much longer, or I would end up in a straightjacket in a rubber room.

Emily got married in April. They had a large ceremony — went all out and spared no expense. The reception was in the ballroom of a hotel. This wedding was much more formal than my roommate's had been, and there were so many people. Mostly people I didn't know. They were coworkers of Emily and her husband, a room full of lawyers. The food consisted of things I had never heard of and was afraid to eat. The cake had five tiers with a perfect bride and groom on top. Emily and her husband received so many gifts they must have needed a moving van to bring everything home. The wedding ended with me catching the bouquet.

After the wedding and reception I disappeared and went for a walk. I felt trapped in that room with all those people. It wasn't just the wedding; I felt trapped in a morbid life. I don't know how long I walked, and I didn't know where I was heading, but I kept walking. I stopped at a park bench and sat for a while. I watched people stroll by. Most of them appeared to be happy except one young woman. She seemed disoriented, and she was mumbling to herself. Maybe like me she was lost in her own sorrow.

I wondered about the happy people. What was their secret, and how had they avoided the mind-numbing dullness of daily life? There were families and lovers who walked by laughing and playing. It was funny how life took its twists and turns, and left people like me dangling on the edge. I felt as if I was drowning beneath the rim of the water. As I sunk lower, the pressure became greater until my lungs felt as though they were being crushed like a soda can beneath a person's foot. The more I tried to swim up to catch my breath, the more the currents pushed me under. I was drowning in my own life.

"Excuse me." Suddenly I heard something that yanked me from my solemn state. A man stopped and asked the time. I had lost track of time, had lost track of my thoughts. He sat down on the bench next to me. He started talking to me, and for some strange reason I found myself talking to him. He seemed somehow familiar. Was it the sound of his voice or his smell? I didn't recognize him. There was something about him though that was inviting. We carried on a conversation for quite some time. I told him about my life, about Nathan. I am not sure why, but I spilled my solitary, lonely life to him. Somehow it felt right, maybe because we were strangers, and I knew I would never see him again. Maybe because he seemed so familiar that I felt I could trust him.

Before we departed he told me, "Life is what you make it. Don't let one setback keep you down." I thought about those words as I walked back to the hotel. That is when I made the decision to take control of my life; to grab on to an anchor and climb up to the water's surface. There were many places I wanted to see and activities I wanted to do. I had compulsively saved money enough to finance a journey. When I got back home I quit my job, moved out of my apartment, and hopped on a bus.

My journey became an exciting chapter in my life that interwove something I had worked hard to forget and put behind me, but somehow I learned to accept and invite back into my life. I remembered the man's words and embraced them wholeheartedly. This was my life, and I was not going to let evil bring me down. I was going to accept the good and learn to live with everything else. I had spent too much time forgetting and starting anew, running away from everything heinous. I wasn't running anymore. I was following a mission I felt compelled to follow. There was something tremendous at the end of my journey waiting for me. The man's voice was so soothing and familiar; I knew there was a reward waiting for me at the end. The reward would be so spectacular that I would know as soon as it happened. It was something I would hold on to for the rest of my days.

The stars were now shining brightly against a moonlit night, and the snow appeared as a blanket of icing across the mountaintop. The woman continued to rock and stare outside as if she were miles above, part of the starry night, looking down at the beauty below.

The Journey

My journey undertook a life of its own. I visited every amusement park, rode every roller coaster, saw every beach my great country had to offer. I went to the top of every mountain, explored every cave, and pondered the beauty of the Grand Canyon. I spent New Year's in Times Square and partied all night during Mardi Gras. I felt as if life were beginning all over again; a new birth that would bring me happiness. I loved the beaches and fresh sea breezes. They seemed so new even though they had existed for millions of years. I collected many shells, at least one from every beach. Each shell had at one time been a creature's home. Now they were washed up on the shore for others to enjoy. I also collected sharks' teeth. In my collection were small black ones, large ones, some that appeared fossilized, and some that were part of a conglomerate of shells.

I loved to sit on the beach during the evening and watch the sun go down beneath the ocean. The sky would turn many shades of red, orange, yellow, and sometimes there were pinks. The chill of the air was inspiring. Many nights I spent sleeping on the beach with my bag as a pillow and my lifelong blanket for covering. I spent many mornings watching the sun rise above the water until it was high in the sky and beating down its harsh rays. On the mountaintops I felt as though I was floating in the clouds. I wanted to reach out and catch one as it drifted by. From the crest of a mountain I could see everything down below; the meandering streams and cozy valleys. There were sparse log cabins that dotted the mountainside. I had not realized there were so many varieties of herbaceous life. Everything was green and blooming. It was amazing that life could survive the harsh, cold, snowy winters on the mountains, but somehow they did, and they appeared fresh and new every spring as soon as the snow melted.

Every night I fell asleep to the stars twinkling in the sky, and I wondered if Cobie was watching the same stars twinkle with me. There was so much beauty in the world that I had never seen until now. I felt I wanted to share it with someone, so I sent postcards to my family and friends, and I kept a journal of all my travels. It wasn't the same as having someone with me — someone to inhale the surrounding exquisiteness, someone to hold and talk with, someone to share my life with.

My entire journey had not been so pleasant, but I absorbed the good with the bad. During one of my stays on the East Coast I encountered what had to be one of the most powerful, destructive forces nature could hurl forth. It had been an almost perfect day when I noticed the sky beginning to change before my eyes. The clouds were rushing over my head; to look at them made me dizzy, and the wind began to pick up. Everything came and went in cycles, every time bringing worse weather. It was breathtaking to watch, but I knew I had to get off the beach and find shelter. I was able to find a room in a cockroach motel with all the windows boarded up. The owner said he was going to ride it out just like the others. He didn't charge me for the room, but told me to stay in, and if the wind picked up real bad to go in the bathroom and close the door. The beach area had become desolate but there were a few who stayed behind. I had been so out of touch with the world around me that I hadn't seen any TV or read any newspapers. I didn't know I was about to be engulfed by something monstrous.

In the motel room I continued to hear the wind and trees as they bent under the power of the storm. I was so curious that I had to go outside and watch. I brought a chair outside my room and stared at what was happening around me. The trees looked flat when a mighty wind gust would come up and push them down. Who knew the wind could be such a bully. The wind would then die down and become calm again;

this went on for a couple of hours. Then the wind became steadier and rain came with it. The rain wasn't normal rain. It went sideways like nothing I had ever seen.

The owner came by to check on me and his property. He yelled that I was sitting outside. He urged me to go back inside because the storm was about to take a very bad turn. I went back inside and listened all night as the wind tossed everything around. I could hear cracking and loud noises, but I wasn't able to make out what they were. I heard the rain pounding on the side of the building. The roof sounded like it was going to blow off, and the electricity went out. I wanted to watch, but I knew I needed to stay in.

At some point I fell into a deep sleep. In my dream I was running on the beach with Nathan. We were playing in the water, splashing each other, and then we were walking along the beach. The sky was a perfect shade of blue, and I could feel the sun's warmth on my body. Abruptly though, the sky changed and turned red. Wind and hail started to pound and beat on us. We ran to find shelter. We ran and ran, but shelter was nowhere. The hotels disappeared, and suddenly Nathan was no longer with me. As soon as he disappeared a school appeared. I ran inside. Inside was Cobie. We held onto each other, and the storm stopped just as abruptly as it had begun. The sky turned a perfect shade of blue once again.

I awoke to pounding on my door. It was the owner checking to make sure I was OK after last night's storm. I got dressed and came outside, and I was amazed to find that everything was calm. The sky was clear blue and told no secrets about last night, but the land told the story. There were tree limbs everywhere, store signs littered the streets, shingles were missing off buildings, and trees had fallen, roots and all, and hit the ground, cars, and buildings. The ground was too soggy to walk on.

It was so desolate it felt like we were the only two people on earth. He made me coffee and breakfast on his camp stove, and we cleaned up around the motel. This seemed like such a normal event in his life, but for me it was exciting, not threatening and scary, as I had pictured hurricanes to be. A few other people came out from other motels and businesses. They had weathered the storm like us and had survived. That evening, the owner, some others, and I all had a bonfire, and I marveled at the sight of the sky. It had gone from surreal blue to half blue and half gold. It was unreal; I had never seen such a sight. Slowly the gold overtook the blue and the sun began to set. The owner called it a tornado sky.

I was beginning to run out of cash, but I had one last place I felt I needed to go and one last thing I needed to do. That is when I headed west and saw the Grand Canyon, and I stopped in the Painted Desert. Afterward, I headed to Las Vegas. Las Vegas was an awe-inspiring sight. There were many bright lights in all varieties of colors including neon. They were flashing and racing before my eyes, inviting me in. It was as if they were saying, *Welcome, friend.* The hotels were huge; each its own mini city.

Inside there were tables set up with blackjack, poker, and roulette. There were slot machines dinging and sirens blaring. Waitresses walked by with trays of drinks, just handing them to people at the tables and the machines. I watched in wonder.

Eventually I made it to the slot machines. I would stay on a machine, win a few dollars and move on. I couldn't afford to lose. Slowly I accumulated $10, $15, $25, but no big cash. I didn't have enough money to try a table. The waitresses kept coming by and handing me drinks, and I began to feel happy and strange. I had never drunk much alcohol before, and maybe should have eaten first, but I didn't care. I kept running into the same people over and over again on the slots, and I must have hit every slot machine in the casino. I decided I might have better luck if I tried a different casino. After I tried several, and my winnings were still meager, I went back to the first. I didn't think I was going to make it as I stumbled along, feeling very light headed and dizzy. I finally made it!

Somehow this made me feel relieved but I had to sit down. When I sat down the room began to spin, so I put my head down and that made it worse. I now felt that my whole body was spinning round and round. I had had too much to drink.

To keep myself anchored, I focused on a man I had seen earlier. He was still at the same machine. I wondered how much money he had fed the machine and if he had won much. As I looked at him more carefully I could see beads of sweat on his forehead and brow. I knew he was losing money, and I assumed he was determined if he played that machine long enough it would somehow give it all back plus more. Once I was feeling better I stumbled over to the machines, keeping my eye on him. I had to know how long he was going to sit at that machine. I slowly played a machine, had a drink, finished my drink, and made it to another machine. He was still there. I could almost see him cussing at the machine in his head. I sat down at one of the bars where I could keep my eye on the man at the machine. Finally, he got up, wiped his face, and moved on.

I got up and slowly made my way to the machine, keeping the man in my sights. He left the casino, and I placed my first quarter in the machine. Before I knew it, lights were flashing and sirens were going off around me. I thought I had broken the machine. All the people came over to me and cheered me on. I couldn't figure out what had happened until one of the casino workers handed me a receipt and told me I had won a double jackpot. I placed the receipt in my pocket, accepted another drink from the waitress, and don't remember any more about that night except some fragmented images of a love long gone.

I woke up in a hotel room the next day feeling like a train had run me over. I put a pillow over my face and pulled up my covers. I didn't know how I had gotten there, but I was inclined not to care. After quite some time, there was a knock at my door. I lay in the bed and didn't move. I felt dead! Then a voice asked how I was doing. The voice—I knew the voice, but I couldn't quite place it, as my brain was still a haze. Was it some stranger from last night? My brain wanted me to get out of bed and answer the door, but my body couldn't move. I was glued to the spot I was in. I remembered that I had won a double jackpot. I felt in my pocket but the receipt wasn't there, just a couple of small bills. What had I done with it? I jumped out of bed and scurried around the room. Again the knock — why wouldn't it go away? I was in panic mode; I had lost all my money. The knock on the door went away. What did they want? Was this room paid for? When the knock went away, and I was sure the coast was clear, I decided to make a quick break and sneak past guest check-in. I grabbed my stuff and exited the room, careful not to seem strange around the people who worked there. I didn't want them to know I was fleeing their hotel without payment.

Once I got out of the hotel, I felt relieved and walked until I was free of the hotel, and then I ran until I couldn't breathe and my side hurt. I found a restaurant and I went in. I didn't have much money, but I had to do something about my pounding headache. I ordered ice water and coffee. The ice water tasted so good, like no ice water had ever tasted before. I drank the whole glass in seconds. I don't think I took one breath until it was finished. I placed loads of sugar and cream in my coffee and sipped on that. Suddenly I had to use the restroom. I guess that is what twelve ounces of water will do. I went to use the restroom, and when I came back to my table, someone was there.

It was a man with long chocolate-brown, wavy hair. I was ready to run again, but when he lifted his head, I recognized his ocean-blue eyes. They came to me in my dreams. I was drawn to his eyes, and then he smiled his half smile with a dimple on the right. This was my reward! The man in the park had given me hope to keep moving on. Somehow that man knew my destiny; my dreams had told me my destiny. I didn't listen then, but this was it. My body took control of my mind, and I came at him with full speed. When he saw me coming he stood up. I wrapped myself around him, and the forward momentum of my body plunging at his almost pushed him backward. This time I planted an open-mouth kiss on him, and it was as magical as the first against the tree in his parents' backyard.

Then I buried my face in his shoulder and cried. I couldn't help it. The tears just ran down my face like Niagara Falls. Everything came flooding back, all the horror of losing Nathan, and how I had always, always loved Cobie. My heart always knew it was Cobie even though I would never accept it. Nathan was a better man with more of a future. He was solid, dependable, and consistent until he left and never came back. What hurt worse than losing Nathan was that my heart truly belonged to Cobie. My heart couldn't accept that. It was torn between these two young men. Nathan was the one who went to war, who fought for our country, and lost his arm doing it. He then was so ashamed he turned himself away from me. I had ruined his life, and it had always been too much of a burden for me to handle. The weight had pushed me down to the lower depths of the ocean and dragged me along.

Cobie, what had Cobie done? Nothing, he was always a smart aleck and was hot and cold. I had my head buried in Cobie's shoulder. I lifted my head and looked around. People were watching us with smiles on their faces. I realized we were in a restaurant. I slowly worked my way off Cobie and sat down. He sat down, put his head in his hands, and laughed. What was so funny?! I kicked him under the table. He looked up at me with his ocean-blue eyes, grabbed my hands under the table, and said, "You seem to be sober now, last night you were on fire." What did he mean on fire, what had I done?

We left the restaurant, and he said he had something important to show me. I got in his truck with him, and we headed out of Las Vegas. I didn't know where we were heading but it felt good to be with him. It felt right. Something in my life finally felt right! I didn't waste any time in asking him what he had meant by *You seem to*

be sober now, last night you were on fire.
He laughed again. I couldn't kick him
this time so I hit him in his side. He said,
"If you stop abusing me I'll be happy to
tell you about last night." That angered
me more and I opened the truck door to
jump out. He stopped the truck, got out,
paced for a while then told me I was
crazy and should get out and walk. I got
out and started walking. He kept on
driving. He made me so mad! What had
happened last night? I tried to
remember but couldn't. There were bits
and pieces, but nothing fit, and I
couldn't make out if it was dream or
reality.

I continued to walk for quite some
time. I was somewhere outside of Las
Vegas but I didn't have a map, any
money, and there appeared to be
nothing for miles. I am not sure how
long I had walked before I finally heard
the sound of an engine. Great, now I
could get a ride. I stood in the middle of
the road, hoping the car would stop.
When it got close enough, I realized it
was Cobie. He stopped and waited. I
wasn't getting back in the truck with

him after he called me crazy because I wanted to know what had happened.

I wasn't crazy! I continued walking. He got out of the truck and walked after me. When he caught up to me, I refused to speak with him. He then told me I was crazier than he thought, because I was walking to nowhere and I would end up dying of hypothermia in the cold, winter night air. I continued to walk, ignoring him even though he was right; as soon as the sun set it would be cold. It wasn't like sleeping on the beach during a warm summer night. The desert got cold. He got back in his truck and cut me off with it, got out, picked me up, and threw me over his shoulder. I was kicking and screaming as he put me back in the truck. He took rope and tied the door handle to the truck bed so I couldn't open it. He wasn't going to lock me in here! I went for the other door but it was locked too. I yelled and screamed that he was the crazy one, trying to run me over and kidnap me!

Who did he think he was to lock me in his truck! These were the reasons I chose Nathan. Nathan would have never locked me in a truck, but he probably would have never gone gambling either. If Nathan hadn't left we would be married now and living in a beautiful brick house with picture windows. There would be stunning flowers bordering the house, accompanied by luscious scents. We would have two children, a boy and a girl, and a pet dog. Our lives would be ideal, not filled with turmoil like being locked in a truck in the desert with a maniac, but that was what attracted me to Cobie the most. He was unpredictable and didn't conform to the ways of society. He was like me.

When I finally settled down he opened his door and got in. He told me to look in the bag behind me. I cautiously opened the bag, expecting something to jump out at me, but nothing happened. Inside the bag were hundreds, no wait, thousands of dollars. Was he a kidnapper and a bank robber? I couldn't say anything; where had all that money come from? He told me the money was mine. So this is where my money went? What was he doing with it? I became angry again, but I kept my cool. I needed to get back to civilization. He calmly explained to me that he had recognized me when I won the jackpot. After I won I proceeded to one of the tables where I started to play. He came over to me, and I kept him there. We played that table for a while, winning, and then I left. He found me later asleep on a couch in one of the bars.

He checked me into a room and went back downstairs to gamble some more. He doubled the money we had already won, and then checked into a room. He then asked me if I had checked my bag. I hadn't thought to check my bag. I already knew what was in it but I opened it up. It looked the same. I felt down to the bottom and pulled out more bundles of cash. He told me I had hidden those last night. I felt relieved knowing this. I hadn't needed to escape the hotel, to feel that I was a criminal on the run. I leaned over and hugged him. We held each other for a while before heading back. I was rich!! We were rich!!!

We went back to Las Vegas and had the time of our lives. We checked into the most elegant hotel in the city. We cleaned up, ate dinner, and went shopping. It was nice to spend money without any worries. I felt like we could do anything and we did. We were on top of the world. Nothing else mattered, and nothing else existed. It was just the two of us. I had never felt exactly this way before. I felt like a girl again and we were still teenagers lost in this exquisite city. We had no responsibilities, no jobs—there was nothing evil that could sneak up on us and make everything come crashing down.

We talked and walked and eventually came to a wedding chapel. It was cute and the flashing sign said open twenty-four hours. We went in, and it was decorated like the rest of the city with bright colors and flashing lights. The people told us what an attractive couple we were, and went through their wedding offers. He asked me to step outside with him. I did. We sat down on a bench, and he asked me to marry him.

He said he loved me and had since high school. My heart dropped, and life stood still. Everything around us stopped. If only I had known how he felt years ago. My life would have been different. Would it have been better though? We were too immature then, and that's why I chose Nathan. He kept me grounded, and I needed that. We were probably too immature now, and I really didn't know much about what he had done the past several years, nor did he know about me. I heard myself say yes. It was as if my heart was working independently of my body and mind. We got married that night and he folded a $100 bill and slid it on my finger as a ring. I never knew a bill could be folded so small, but I never gave up that bill or stopped wearing it.

As the elderly lady rocked, the snow sparkled in the starry moonlit night, and she once again shifted her gaze; this time downward toward her lap where she had her hands folded.

Home Again

Our marriage followed the same tumultuous path from which it had come. It was like a roller coaster, always up and down. We would fight, and Cobie would get so angry. I could always tell when he was upset, and would anger him more. He would pace, run his fingers through his hair, mumble about how frustrating and insane I was, and then he'd go for a walk. No matter how cold or hot, he would go for a walk. I would ignore him, which angered him more. Sometimes I would comment back, and other times I was the first to anger. I believe we fought on purpose. We somehow enjoyed watching the other become irritated. After, when he would come back, we would wrap our arms around each other and hold on for life. I enjoyed the security of his arms, and I loved the smell of his body. He would tell me how beautiful I was and remind me just how much he loved me.

He always said I was even more beautiful when I was upset, which infuriated him more. Our partnership became stronger with every battle. We understood each other better and became more dependent on the other. I knew he couldn't live without me and I couldn't even imagine life without him. He was my life, and no matter what he or I said to cause sorrow to the other, we knew love was behind it.

The first year we invested our money, made more, and traveled the world. We had made thousands that night in Vegas, and we decided to invest some of it. We learned to play the stock market. Cobie was clever and had common sense. I had skills with numbers that I never thought would pay off. Together we made hundreds of thousands of dollars. We traveled to places we had only dreamed of and almost every continent. We went to Italy, Japan, and to China to see the Great Wall. We went exploring in Australia, Africa, and South America. I had never seen such animals except in textbooks and on TV. We respected other cultures, and we valued what we could learn from them. The world was full of splendor and surprises everywhere.

Like me, Cobie had no definitive home. He had held many jobs. He had been a handyman, plumber, gardener, and mechanic. His home was his truck. Mine was my bag of goodies that I had collected from everywhere and my journal of all my travels. None of our items meant much to anybody else, but they meant home to us. We went where life took us with no path. We were leaves in the wind, and we went wherever we were blown. The honeymoon finally ended when my parents contacted me, asking me to come home. My dad had recently retired, and they wanted to travel and visit people they hadn't seen for years, and they wanted to see me. I hadn't told them I was married, and I didn't want them hurt. My life had taken such a twist, and everything happened so quickly. We had no responsibilities except each other, and now we had to come back down to earth and face our families and friends. We went back home. The trip back was solemn; neither of us said much. I felt like a child being reprimanded by my parents for staying out too late. I felt selfish for doing everything wonderful I wanted to do instead of thinking about my family. My parents meant a lot to me, and they had always been there for me—but where had I been—nowhere but everywhere.

Back home, nothing had changed. The town looked the same; my parent's house looked the same. It was as if I was stuck in a time warp and had traveled back several years into the past. I was now a teenager again, and Cobie was the boy who exasperated me to no end. I was mad at him, but I couldn't explain to myself why. I kicked him for no reason except to kick him. He grabbed me and kissed me. I tried to pull away, but his grasp was too strong. He knew me sometimes better than I knew myself; maybe because we were the same. My parents rushed out the door with their arms open. It felt so good to be held by them again. The tears welled up in my eyes, and I felt butterflies in my belly. How could I tell them I had gotten married?

We all walked inside and sat down in the living room. My mom was so full of talk. She had so many questions to ask and stories to tell me. I knew she and my dad had been worried about me while I traveled. They seemed relieved that Cobie was with me and didn't ask any questions. Cobie left for a while and I just reminisced with my parents. I told them about my travels and showed them all my trinkets in my bag.

They filled me in on everything that had happened; how Mr. Fur had died, and they buried her in a proper grave in the backyard. Mr. Fur had been my friend through my darkest hours. She was always there, and she cuddled at my feet and purred in my face. I had loved Mr. Fur, and I cried at the thought of her dying without me. How had I stayed gone so long? My mother told me that Emily was pregnant, that Sammy had gotten married and moved back into town, and how Carry had been killed by a hit-and-run driver. The police never found out who did it. I had never liked Carry and thought she was evil in human form, but I never would have wished death on her; I had never even thought such a horrible thing.

We reap what we sew in life, and Carry stabbed everyone in the back including Rebecca, her best and most personal friend. I had thought their evilness was inseparable, but Carry had found a way in our senior year of high school to make Rebecca's life horrible. Rebecca fought back though, and Carry came out looking like a fool. It had happened over a young man. Carry had been dating him, but she threw him away like she threw everyone else away. Rebecca began dating him a few months later. It didn't seem strange. Almost every good-looking boy in school was Carry's used trash, and Rebecca and Carry dated many of the same boys—share and share alike. Evidently Carry had feelings for this one, but it was Rebecca he had feelings for. Maybe she didn't so much have feelings for him but, she couldn't accept how he favored Rebecca over her. Carry was always the star, she always at the top of every conversation. She didn't like anyone else to steal the spotlight or infringe on her stardom.

The rumor went that he broke up with Carry, but she played it off that she had been the one to end the relationship. There is no way she could let the student body know that someone had dumped her. The rumor also went that he had dumped her because he found out that he was just a part of a bet. Carry, Jules, Regina, and Jennifer all had made a bet that each could date, dump, and move on to more boys than the other. They couldn't date the same boy twice, but they could date more than one boy at a time. It was a cutthroat competition and Carry, being the most heartless, would have stopped at nothing and would never have been able to live up to someone else doing the dumping. Rebecca, not being part of the competition, led me to believe that she had a heart and wasn't quite as malicious as I had previously thought.

Whatever the reason it started, Rebecca had his attention. Carry became furious, releasing her fiery anger on him and Rebecca. She started rumors about them, saying the cruelest things. Carry had a way of stirring everything up at school. All the students both feared her and loved her at the same time, and nobody but nobody ever double-crossed her. We all knew there would be a price to pay if we did. Rebecca paid that price, but she proved herself to be just as powerful as Carry, and the student body was split. It was a war that ended in a draw when we graduated and went off to college. The world was probably a better place without her. Maybe, just maybe it wasn't a hit-and-run.

 After a few hours, Cobie came back. He had always had perfect timing. My dad had just walked outside. I saw Cobie and my father talking. I wondered what they were talking about. Was Cobie telling my father that he and I were married? That wasn't his place to do so; it was mine, and I didn't know how to tell them without breaking their hearts. I wanted so much to run out there and kick Cobie in the shins, but I refrained. Instead, I watched and had a difficult time focusing on what my mom was saying. I tried so hard to focus on her and him at the same time. I was distracted. Finally my dad gave Cobie a hug. My father didn't just hand out hugs to other men unless they were family. He had told him! I was furious!

They walked to the garage, chatting like old buddies. When my father came in, I stole the opportunity to go to the garage and talk with Cobie. Really, I wasn't going to talk but yell softly. I immediately accused him of telling my father. He laughed, the way he did when I accused him of things, or I got upset over something he thought was silly. It wasn't silly! The closest thing to me was an empty plastic flower pot. I threw it at him and missed. My aim was always horrible, and his reflexes were always too quick for me to get in a successful shot, but I really didn't want to hit him. I just wanted him to know how displeased I was. Now he was angry, pacing and mumbling to me how I was paranoid and always thought the worst of him. He walked off to his truck and sat in it for a while. I held my ground, and I stayed where I was. I was in the right and knew it. He was wrong.

After what seemed like an eternity, he came back with something cuffed in his hand. He came up to me and knelt down, risking the chance that I would kick him, and he proposed to me again. He handed me a beautiful diamond ring. I didn't understand. Weren't we already married? I looked into his clear blue eyes and could see his sincerity. I said yes all over again. He hadn't told my father we were married. He had asked my father's permission to marry me. My father had granted that permission. Cobie always infuriated me so much, and he was right; I did always think the worst of him. He was really and truly a very sentimental and sensitive person. I held him and cried on his shoulder. How could I be so cruel and throw a flower pot at him? We never did tell my parents or anybody else that we had gotten married in Las Vegas. It was our little secret.

The next few days I helped my parents pack for their trip. I stayed with my parents, and Cobie stayed with his.

Nobody questioned anything; they believed we were engaged. My parents were planning a trip that would last a few months, ending with them visiting Emily in time for their first grandchild to be born, and they asked me to house sit. I couldn't turn them down.

Over the next few months I rekindled my relationship with Sammy. She had gotten married and moved back. I hadn't spoken with her since I went into my depression. I had forced everybody out of my life then, but now I felt ready to face anything. Cobie gave me that strength and made me want to fight not just him but the world. He made me alive again. Sammy and I both reverted back to our childhood together. We had slumber parties, went shopping, and talked about our spouses, only she didn't realize I was married to mine. She helped me plan my wedding and choose a wedding dress. She had welcomed me back without any questions. She had known me so well that she didn't need to ask any questions. She shared her life and adventures with me, and I shared mine with her.

Sammy, her husband, and Cobie and I all got along well; in fact, sometimes it scared me that we did. Cobie and Sammy's husband, Clay, were so much alike. They were like two little boys together with mischievous minds. Sammy and her husband both worked, unlike Cobie and me. We had what seemed like an unlimited amount of money, although we lived inexpensively and really didn't need much. Our amusement didn't come from material items but from each other.

A lot of new construction seemed to be springing forth since our arrival and we spent time visiting model homes, driving around, and going to open houses. It filled the time, and Cobie seemed especially interested. To me it just killed time. Other days I didn't know what Cobie did. He seemed preoccupied with something. One morning he came by early, extremely early. The sun wasn't even up. He told me not to say anything, but to pack my clothes because we were going on a trip for a couple of days. I was too tired to be angry, argue, or hit him with something.

I did what he asked. Normally I would have put up a fight. We got in his truck, and we headed out of town. I really had no idea where we were going, but thought I would give Cobie this one and allow him to surprise me.

The trip was quiet, and my mind wandered. I wondered why, with all our money, he was still driving this old junker truck. The paint was faded to a very light shade of an orangey red like rust, and the driver's side seat was so worn that the springs popped out. That couldn't have been comfortable to sit on. There was no carpet in the truck, just metal floorboards. The dash was cracked from one end to the other, and the driver's side door didn't open easily. To open it from the outside, the door had to be lifted slightly and the button not pushed in until the door was raised to the correct elevation. It seemed impossible to me to open it from the inside, but he always managed. The truck was in perfect mechanical condition though, and Cobie loved this vehicle. It was his first love, the truck his grandfather had left to him. I always came second to the truck.

I must have dozed off because when I woke up we were at a gas station somewhere in the foothills. Cobie was nowhere that I could see, and I slowly, drowsily got out of the truck and stretched. The sun was shining brightly and there were remnants of snow on the ground. I looked around, and I saw a picturesque little town nestled in the foothills. When Cobie came back, he had breakfast for us, got back in the truck, and started the engine without saying a word. I jumped back in the truck, and I saw such a serious look on his face. He seemed very preoccupied with something. I mentioned about how quaint the town was and how beautiful the scenery. He mumbled words in agreement and continued to drive. If he wasn't going to talk, I was going to listen to something on the radio. I changed his station that had been playing quietly through the whole trip, and to my amusement, he didn't stop me or say anything. He usually didn't like me to fool with buttons and knobs in his truck. He was acting very strangely, and he wouldn't even put up a fight.

We drove up the foothills and up the mountain. It took hours, and my ears popped with the elevation. He pulled into a narrow driveway that appeared to go nowhere. Finally it ended in a small cabin. It looked like a painting. The cabin had two windows in the front and a door in between. There were two rocking chairs sitting out front and a small round table. He got out a key, and we went inside. The cabin smelled like spring inside. The smell seemed so out of place for winter on the top of this mountain, and my nose followed the fresh springy smell to the kitchen table where fresh cut flowers sat in a vase. There weren't flowers for miles, and I wondered how they had gotten on the table. It was the cutest cabin I had ever seen, but why were we here and inside? Weren't we trespassing?

He finally asked me what I thought. I thought it was breathtaking, especially the view from the front. The whole mountainside could be seen. I could see the valley below and many other small cabins that clung to its side. He came over and held me in his arms, and I didn't ask why we were here. I didn't want to ruin the moment; the two of us standing here in this picture-perfect cabin. We were the only two people. I simply stated it was beautiful. He told me that it was mine. That night in the cabin we conceived something tremendous between us, something that turned our lives upside down.

The next day was the first day of the rest of our lives. We explored the area on foot. We were running and playing like children, hiding in and out of the huge trees. The trees must have been hundreds of years old. I found one that had been hollowed out like the one in my dream years ago. I went inside and it was just big enough for me to fit into. I sat down and closed my eyes. When I did, I saw Nathan smiling at me, offering me his hand. In my vision I went with him and we floated above the mountains. I could see Cobie and me below, running around, acting silly.

Then I saw another face that looked like Cobie's. The face had the same clear blue eyes and the same dimple as Cobie but it wasn't Cobie. Unlike Cobie he had golden-colored hair. This face turned into a person, a young person who was laughing and playing with us. It was like a fantasy world, and I felt so at peace. My whole being was calm and serene. When I opened my eyes Nathan had disappeared and Cobie was there. The snow started to fall lightly, and we made snow angels in front of the cabin. That evening after dinner we sat in the twin rocking chairs with the fire roaring behind us in front of the window, held hands as we rocked, and watched the snow fall as we planned our future. We had never thought into the future before; we had always lived in the here and now. But that night we planned. Cobie's father was selling his auto shop, and Cobie wanted to buy it from him.

Two weeks after our trip to the cabin my parents came home. They were so excited to tell me about Emily's babies, their grandchildren. I was unaware that babies did more than eat, sleep, cry, and poop, but evidently they did when they were yours. My niece and nephew, twins, were tiny and bald, but cute in a strange way. They had named them Trent and Tansey. Cobie, true to his word, had bought his father's shop. I guess we were here to stay. No more traveling the world on a whim. I had a secret that I had kept quiet from everyone including Cobie. I had decided to surprise him on our "wedding night." My secret was just another reason to make a home.

We got married again. It was a small but elegant wedding. After the wedding, when Cobie and I were alone, I told him my secret. He didn't seem surprised at all. This didn't seem to anger me though. Since our weekend at the cabin my entire perspective on life was distorted. I was calm, happy, and almost melancholy at times. He had noticed this change in me. We didn't go on a honeymoon since we'd been honeymooning since we got married. Instead, we found and bought a house.

The house we bought became our home, and we enjoyed many happy

years of our lives in that house. It was a
Spanish-style stucco home. There was a
large patio in the front covered by an
awning supported by curved stucco
arms. Inside there was an entryway
shrouded in windows. The entryway
stepped down into a great room, and
there was a fireplace on the far wall.
True to the style of the house the
entryways into every room were
curved. Stemming from the great room
were three entries to other rooms and a
sliding glass door that led outside to a
large covered patio. The entry to the left
of the great room led to the bedrooms.
There was a short hallway with two
bedrooms on one side, with a bathroom
in between, and a master bedroom and
bath on the other side. To the right of
the great room, one of the entries went
to a half bath and the garage, and the
other went to the kitchen. The kitchen
was large, and it included a dining area.
There was a bar that separated the
kitchen from the great room and
another sliding glass door that led
outside to the covered patio. At the end
of the covered patio was a built-in

swimming pool, surrounded by more patio and grass around the patio. We had a large yard with a couple of very old large trees. We had found the house while looking at homes during one of our expeditions. I had fallen in love with its charm and potential, and it became our home.

The elderly woman continued to rock and look outside at the piles of snow fallen earlier in the night. It was as if there was something in the snow drawing her gaze toward it.

Nine Months

The next nine months of my life were incredible. I didn't understand until now how having a baby growing inside me could be so exciting and difficult at the same time. We hadn't planned this baby. God had planned this baby. He had chosen to bless us and to make us a complete little family. Cobie and I didn't care whether this baby was a boy or a girl. We just wanted this baby to be healthy. I took my vitamins daily in the recommended amounts. Cobie and I went for long walks together after work. The doctor had said walking was the best exercise, and it would help my labor when the time came. We read to the baby and talked to the baby. Cobie told him about servicing a car, and I told to him about finances. Cobie loved to put his hands on my belly and feel the baby move. Sometimes he would lay his head on my belly and sing softly. I would rub my belly or sometimes just hold my belly. I loved to feel the baby.

Our families couldn't have been happier, but they all had their opinions on whether the baby was a boy or a girl. They had opinions on what we should name the baby. My parents already had two grandchildren, but they were still as excited about this one as they had been about Emily's. Cobie's parents didn't have any grandchildren. He was an only child. This baby had seemed a second chance for them, whereas my parents were much calmer. Everybody wanted what was best for this baby.

The first trimester of my pregnancy was probably the worst. I had no appetite. All the food I used to love seemed extremely unappetizing. I had an incredible urge though for water, soda crackers, and milk. I didn't just want to drink milk but white milk, and I went through about three to four gallons a week by myself. I had never really liked white milk. I had always drunk it with chocolate, and now I wanted it plain and white. I knew this baby was going to have strong bones. The smells of food cooking made me sick to my stomach. I never got sick or had morning sickness; I just felt nauseous all day long. I would get dizzy spells as well. Everything would start to go black and I would have to sit down. I didn't feel like myself. It was like someone else had taken over my body. I felt very calm and serene, like I was floating on a cloud. I felt tired at the oddest times, and I would lie down for a nap. Cobie would usually lie beside me, and he'd rub his fingers through my hair and under my hair. Then he would caressingly massage my back. At night the only way I could sleep was to curl up against Cobie's back and breathe in time with his breathing. As soon as our breathing was in sync, I would fall asleep. It was an exciting time. I was able to hear the baby's heart beat at the end of my first trimester. I went to the doctor once a month, and Cobie insisted on coming with me. Together we heard our baby's heartbeat.

My second trimester was more pleasant. I had gotten over my loss of appetite, and I wanted to eat everything. I ate and ate like I had a bottomless pit. After I finished eating, I would eat more within about an hour. I didn't gain much weight though. I wasn't sure where all the food went but it didn't show. I had gotten over my nausea and dizzy spells. I still drank a lot of water and milk though. I started having strange aches and pains in my legs and back. It felt like someone took a needle and injected something into me. The pains in my legs would shoot down my leg, starting from my hip and ending at my toes. The pains in my back were duller pains. Sometimes I would even feel short, sharp pains in my chest.

I could feel the baby starting to move. At first it was little kicks. Then it felt like the baby wasn't just kicking, but it was balling up its fists and hitting. One morning I woke up to a sharp pain that started in my chest and worked its way down through my belly. I could see the baby turn all the way around in my belly. The baby had done a somersault. My belly felt like it was being stretched, and I could see the outline of the baby as it turned in my belly. My belly had become horribly distorted, and it hurt. I started to rub my belly, and the baby seemed to calm down. Cobie's excitement grew with each passing day.

At night when we were relaxing, we would sprawl out on the couch with my back against his chest. He would place his arms around me, with his hands on my belly, and feel the baby kick. Sometimes the baby would start hiccupping. The kicks were random, but the hiccups followed a pattern. Cobie had gotten used to me sleeping with my chest to his back, and he enjoyed feeling the little kicks the baby would give and the hiccups. The baby seemed though to think it was time to be playful and active, and I couldn't sleep. I started lying on my other side, and then the baby went right to sleep with me. Cobie would then snuggle up against my back, and he'd place his hand on my chest.

My third trimester was the most exciting. I began eating smaller amounts, but I was eating very frequently. I had kept a refrigerator in my office at the shop, and I would snack all day long. The pains I had started feeling occasionally during my last trimester got worse, and they happened more often. Sometimes, as I was walking, my legs would give out under me. Cobie stayed very close to my side. He was afraid I was going to fall and that the baby and I would be hurt. The baby and I had already formed a bond. I knew when the baby was ready to play, sleep, or just wanted to be talked to. The baby seemed to talk to me with the movements it would make in my belly.

Cobie and the baby had seemed to make a connection as well. There were times when the baby seemed to get excited when Cobie would put his hands on my belly. I wasn't sure how the baby knew his hands from mine, but the baby seemed to. I could be holding my belly or gently rubbing it and the baby would be calm, and then Cobie would talk to the baby or put his hands on my belly, and the baby would start doing somersaults. I felt very hot and would sleep with the window open, even on very cold nights. Cobie would be bundled in bed with three covers over him to stay warm. After I was asleep he would try to sneak the covers over me as well, but I would grow too hot and kick them off in my sleep. It was becoming more difficult for me to sleep. I would toss and turn all night, and then I'd wake up feeling tired. My belly had turned into a round ball, and I could feel the baby very low. Sometimes I was afraid the baby was going to just drop out, especially after I would get sharp pains stemming from the top of my belly and ending in my abdomen. I had gained about twenty-five pounds by the end of my third trimester.

My mother and Cobie's mother decided to have a baby shower for me. I received so many gifts, clothes, diapers, a stroller, baby wipes, baby toys, blankets, a bassinet—and from my parents and Cobie's—a crib, dresser, and changing table. Cobie and his father loaded everything into his truck for us to take home. After the shower, Cobie painted the walls in the room a mint green, he bought me a rocking chair, and then he set up the crib, dresser, and changing table. I unpacked all the other various gifts and found homes for them. As the time grew closer, my realization that I was going to be a mother became more genuine. Cobie and I packed an overnight bag and waited.

The day finally happened. I had slept perfectly the night before, and I woke up once to use the restroom. When I woke up, I went to the bathroom, sat on the toilet, and my water broke. I didn't know what had happened at first. It was an involuntary action. When it struck me what had happened, I woke up Cobie. He called the hospital, and they said for him to bring me in. The baby was already two weeks late. I wasn't in a hurry though. I felt great, better than I had felt in weeks. I felt so calm and relaxed. I felt like I could just have the baby at home. After two incredibly uncomfortable weeks of waiting, I felt great; this time I was going to make the baby wait just a bit. I asked Cobie to make me breakfast. He seemed a little disturbed, but he made me breakfast. After I ate he told me to get dressed because we were going to the hospital.

As soon as we got out the door my water started leaking again. I had lost so much in the toilet, I didn't know there was any more to lose. I was leaking all over his truck. He had a towel behind the seat, and he gave it to me to sit on. When we got to the hospital they had a room waiting for me. Cobie had already called our parents. He used the time while I was eating. The first thing they did was make me take off my clothes; my pants were soaked anyway, and it felt good to get out of them. They made me put on a horrible robe with no back. I had better gowns in my bag but they wouldn't let me wear them. Then they checked to see how far I was dilated. I was at one centimeter. Next they asked me questions about me labor pains. How often did I have them, and how long did they last? While one nurse was asking me questions, another was hooking up a device to monitor the baby's heartbeat. They hooked up another device to monitor my labor pains, how often and how long they occurred.

They kept coming back every hour to check to see how much I was dilated. I went from one centimeter to three, then four, and then six. The baby's heartbeat stayed steady, and they said my labor was progressing smoothly. My labor pains didn't seem to hurt. I was prepared for them to be painful, but they weren't. My stomach just felt like it was tightening up, and then it was releasing. When they checked on me the next hour, I hadn't dilated any farther; I was stuck at six centimeters. For the next several hours I didn't dilate any farther. I felt trapped in the hospital, in this bed with machines hooked to me. I couldn't walk around, because my gown had no back, and I didn't know how to unhook the machines. I was miserable. I had known we didn't need to be in such a hurry to leave, but I didn't want to argue with Cobie. I knew the look he gave me, and he was very serious about leaving. I thought that maybe the baby had second thoughts about being born. Now I was stuck to this bed, uncomfortable, and getting angry.

The hospital had allowed our parents in the room. My mom sat beside me, and she gave me encouraging words, but I felt really gross. Cobie left

the room for a while. When he came
back, they said I could change my gown
and take a walk around the hospital.
They unhooked me from the machines,
and I changed my gown. Next Cobie
and I walked for a while. When we
came back to the room everything was
hooked back up, and they checked to
see if I had dilated. I was still at six. The
next time they came back I was at eight,
and they told me it was time. They
wheeled me out of my room and placed
me in another. The nurses told me to
push. I didn't feel like pushing, and I
wasn't sure when I was supposed to
push. I had never done this before. They
told me to push when I had a
contraction. I still didn't really feel the
contractions, but had learned to read the
machine. I had formed a relationship
with it since being hooked to it all day. I
started pushing and the doctor came in.
I guess the baby was ready to make its
debut in the world after all. I pushed,
and every time the baby would turn its
head. The doctor would reach in with
his hand to turn the baby's head back,
but then when I pushed, the baby would

turn its head again. The doctor finally said that he might have to use forceps if the baby moved its head the next time. The baby didn't move its head the next time, and I could see its head and hair. The baby had brown hair. The baby was finally coming out! The doctor checked the baby's head. After that, I pushed one more time, and our baby came all the way out. Cobie cut the umbilical cord, and I held the baby in my arms on my chest for as long as I could. He was so tiny. Then they took the baby to a small table with a light on in the corner to check the baby's vitals. The baby started to cry. They said the baby was a healthy baby boy.

They took the baby to the nursery to clean him up and finish with me. Cobie left with them to look at his newborn son and show our parents which beautiful baby was their grandson. The nurses pressed on my stomach, and they asked if it hurt. Well of course it hurt! I just had a baby. As they pressed on my belly, the placenta came gushing out. As they worked on me and talked, I thought of the baby. I wanted to hold him again. After they were finished with me, they told me to get some rest, and then they left.

I was all alone. How could I rest? I had been surrounded by people all day, checking on me, checking on the baby. Cobie and our parents had been there. Now I was all alone. Didn't I matter anymore? I wasn't tired. I wanted my baby and someone to be here with me, but I was alone. After what seemed like an eternity, but was probably more like ten to fifteen minutes, my mom came in. It was like she had read my mind. She said he was a beautiful baby and I had done a great job. She sat with me, holding my hand until I fell asleep. When I woke up, Cobie was with me. He said they were getting ready to bring the baby in for his first feeding. I was so excited. When they brought him in, I remembered how small he was. I held him in my arms, and the nurse showed me how to feed him. He didn't seem hungry; he just wanted to be held in his mother's arms.

It was nine months after we were married that our son was born. We named him Jacob after his father, grandfather, and great-grandfather. Jacob was Cobie's true name, but he had always been called Cobie because there were so many Jacobs in the family. Like Cobie's parents, we didn't call our son Jacob. We called him Reese. He was born two weeks late, and nobody expected that he hadn't been conceived on our "wedding" night.

The elderly lady still rocking continued to stare outside at the snow. Her gaze seemed immovable as she looked out through the window at the hills of snow that covered the mountaintop.

Reese

Reese had changed our lives forever. It was no longer Cobie and me, but Cobie, Reese, and me. We were a whole and complete little family. Reese was born with a full head of brown hair, which he later shed, and he grew in chestnut-colored hair. His eyes were a deep blue that over the years lightened to an ocean blue like his father's. He looked like his father except for his hair. He was the boy Nathan had shown me running and playing at the cabin with us. He had a quiet demeanor, but he had a curiosity about the world. We had to keep a close eye on him at all times. He was the center of our lives and Daddy's little boy.

Reese was a mini Cobie in every way, from how he smiled to how he reacted when he became upset. He was so funny to watch when he got mad. When he was a baby, he would burble at us and crawl away and sulk, only to come back for hugs and kisses. When he grew older, he would mumble quietly under his breath and go sit outside and sulk, only to come back in and apologize. When he was a baby, we brought him to work with us. Cobie kept up the mechanic end of the shop and I did the finances. Reese would stay in the office with me when he was a baby, but as he grew more curious he would wander out into the shop, and Cobie would prop him up and explain to him what he was working on. They were inseparable, and Reese admired his father more than any other human alive. He and Cobie spent almost every waking hour together. After Reese started school, Cobie insisted on picking him up from school and bringing him back to the shop with us. I think it was harder on Cobie when Reese started school than it was on me.

By the time Reese was ten, he could take an engine apart and put it back together. He was just as clever as his father. Once, when Reese was 11, Cobie went to pick him up from school as usual, but they didn't come back right away. At first I didn't worry, because sometimes he would take him to get ice cream, a hamburger, or to see his grandparents, but after three hours I started to worry and panic. My stomach became all knotted up inside, and I couldn't stay in the shop, so I left. I went home first, but they weren't there. Next I stopped at my parents', because sometimes Cobie would bring Reese over there after school, as his grandparents loved to spend time with him, but they weren't there either. Next I tried Cobie's parents' house, but they weren't home.

I drove everywhere I could think of that they might be, and I tried places I didn't think they would be. They were nowhere to be found. I finally went back to the shop, and there they were with every mechanic in the shop marveling over a heap of metal. To them it was gold. To me it was a frame and body of some long-forgotten, dilapidated piece of ……I ran over to Reese, and I hugged him and yelled at Cobie for not calling to tell me they were OK or where they were — right there in front of everyone. He looked at me like I was insane and walked off. Reese seemed confused at why I was mad at Daddy. He gave me a puzzling look. He didn't seem to care though. He was so excited because Daddy had bought the heap of metal for him. They were going to rebuild it together. I guess it was some type of male bonding exercise. Cobie and I didn't speak until later that night, and he apologized. He said this time I was right. He should have called. Reese and his father spent hours on that car. It was their hobby, and they shared it. Sometimes I felt left out.

While Cobie taught Reese about being a man, I taught Reese about the rest of the world. When he was a baby, I read stories to him. When he was tired, it was my lap that he laid his head on. When he fell out of the tree, got bitten by a snake and had to be rushed to the emergency room, and when he flipped over the handlebars of his bike, I was the one whose shoulder he cried on. I wanted him to know his grandparents, and I encouraged any opportunities he had to spend with them. I had wonderful memories of my grandparents, and I wanted him to have wonderful memories of his. When it was time for him to learn to use the potty, I taught him how to not be afraid. I told him when he peed he would make the water change color. That interested him, and he laughed every time and shouted that he had turned it "geen." When he was little he thought it was great.

When it was time for him to go to school, I bought him two backpacks, one for home and one for school. He would fill his home backpack with his toys, sometimes bugs, and usually tools. We had to check his school backpack every morning to make sure he didn't sneak any tools to school. When he first started school, I would volunteer to help out so he didn't think he had to be there alone, and so I could make sure he didn't have any teachers like Boogie Woman. I read many stories to him from my journal, and the hurricane was always his favorite. I knew I had my place in Reese's life, but I couldn't help being a little envious of Cobie and Reese. They talked cars together and sports together, and I could have joined in. Working in the shop I had the knowledge of cars, and working around men all day I had the knowledge of sports and other manly interests, but I gave them their special time and I took my special time. I enjoyed every minute that I had to spend with Reese.

Reese had two loves in life; the first cars and the second bugs. He spent many waking hours tinkering on his car at the shop. He would work at the shop, and we paid him. Most of the money he made he put into the car. It went from a heap of metal to a metallic blue sports car. They transformed the interior into showroom quality with rich leather seats and a chrome instrument panel. The engine sounded like a V8. It rumbled and shook the walls. All the chrome shone so brightly that when the sun hit it directly the light reflected off, and it was blinding to the eyes. He loved this car, and he had done most of the work himself with Cobie's help. It took them five years to get it to the showroom quality that they strived for. His talents weren't just in the mechanics of a vehicle but also the appearance.

Switching out a seat or installing a wiring harness was no problem for him. He didn't just use his talents to work on his own car either. He used them to make his dad's truck better.

Cobie was very attached to his truck and didn't like anybody to mess with it, but Reese was the exception to that rule. Reese put in a new bench seat; he carpeted the floorboards, put in a new dash and instrument panel, and reupholstered the ceiling. He installed a state-of-the-art stereo and speakers, and when he was finished with all that he painted it a cherry red. He did this little by little and never with any help. He refused help because he wanted to do it on his own for his dad.

Reese also had a curiosity of the world about him, and he loved bugs. I knew that if he didn't take over the shop when he grew up, he would become an entomologist. He collected bug specimens, placed them in glass jars, and poked holes in the lids. He would sometimes keep the bugs for days, studying their habits. He made us buy him a bug encyclopedia, and he could name every bug he found. I made him keep the bugs in the garage or outside where, in my opinion, they belonged. Sometimes though he would get so excited about some new bug he found that he would come running into the house to show us.

One weekend Cobie decided to build Reese a tree house to keep all his bugs in. Reese got so excited. They measured the dimensions of the biggest tree in our backyard, and then they headed to the lumber store. They cut, pounded, and worked all weekend from dawn to dusk, and when they were finished, it wasn't just a tree house but a tree mansion. Cobie also bought him a microscope so he could more closely study his bugs. Reese was in heaven, and he would spend many hours in his tree mansion, which soon became his laboratory.

Reese had a best friend, Vince. Vince lived across the street and down a couple of doors. He was the same age as Reese. He was just as curious as Reese about bugs, and he became his laboratory partner. They explored their yards and the neighborhood together, collecting bugs. When they were older, they rode their bikes to the park, other neighborhoods, and friends' houses in search of bugs. They were like the bug patrol. When they were about 12, they started a lawn business. I think it was a way for them to explore and find bugs in more people's yards, but whatever the reason, it kept them busy and they made money. They would sometimes have competitions to see who could mow the most lawns and collect the most money.

Reese also fixed everybody's lawn equipment in the neighborhood. Sometimes he not only fixed it but improved it. My neighbors had superpowered lawn equipment. We had bought a riding mower to take to the cabin with us. The grass was always overgrown in the spring and summer, and Reese turned it into a powered drag racing mower.

Reese tried to show Vince how to work on engines, but Vince had no mechanical abilities. He couldn't even fix his bike when it was broken. He would always take it to Reese. Vince had other talents though; he could draw. He loved comics, collected them, and made his own. Reese had talked him into entering a comic book contest, and Vince did. He won first place. Reese was proud of his friend. Each had his own talents. Reese could fix and improve anything mechanical, and Vince could draw. They were best friends, and Vince was almost like a second son. We even loved him like a second son.

Reese and his two older cousins didn't get along well. Trent and Tansey, in my opinion, were brats. We mostly had to see them on the holidays. Trent and Tansey—or T and T, as I called them—were, as their nickname implied, explosive. They were adorable children with golden ringlets, emerald-green eyes, and they looked like little angels, but their looks were deceiving. They were really little heathen children. I didn't like to think that way about my niece and nephew, but they were horrible. They had gone through so many nannies when they were toddlers that my sister had to stop working to take care of them. They were sneaky and conniving.

When they were all little, Reese admired them and wanted to hang out with them, but somehow he was the one who came out looking guilty. One Christmas they fed my mom's dog, which my dad had given her for Christmas the year before, champagne. After they got the dog drunk, Reese was the one chasing him around trying to play, and then the dog got sick all over the floor. Another year they dug up my mom's flower bulbs. Reese was the one covered in dirt because he was trying to rebury them. He knew how much Grandma loved her flowers, and how upset she would be when she saw the bulbs laying all over the ground. Another year they were all playing ball, and Trent hit the ball through the window of a neighbor's house. T and T ran inside, leaving Reese behind. One year when they were all really little, T and T took Reese's toys that my parents had at their house and tried to flush them down the toilet. Instead, the toilet overflowed and made a huge mess. Everybody always knew it was T and T that were responsible, but Reese always felt bad.

When T and T went to school, my sister and her husband decided to have another child before she took up her career again. Their third child, they named Trey. He was nothing like T and T. He was quiet, calm, and loved Reese. After he was born, Reese stopped hanging out with T and T, and he took care of Trey. He began to protect Trey from his demonic siblings. Once when Trey was just an infant and taking his afternoon nap, T and T snuck in the room and took him out of bed. Reese knew they were up to something, and he was old enough and smart enough to know they were up to no good; he didn't want to get into trouble. He came running to me and told me they were in the baby's room. I followed him, and we found Trey in a laundry basket covered in clothes. I picked up Trey and took him to my sister. She seemed puzzled. I told her what her little heathens had done. That was the first time I saw T and T get into any real trouble. I'm not sure how Trey survived at home. Maybe it was the twins being sent to military school. They were so bad they had gotten kicked out of every private school in their area. My sister and her husband decided the twins needed a behavior adjustment.

Reese wasn't just the apple of our eyes but his grandparents' eyes as well. We lived close to both Cobie's parents and mine. Reese had many opportunities to spend with them. Cobie's father showed him how to do complete car restorations. Before the earthquake and Cobie's family moved here, his dad worked for a car restoration shop. He passed on this knowledge to Reese, who perfected it into a talent. Cobie's mother spent time with him and his bugs. I think he acquired his love for bugs from her. She had a huge butterfly collection that Reese marveled over. He wasn't interested though in preserving bugs, just studying them.

My parents had a special liking for Reese. He was their favorite grandchild, even though they would never admit it. Maybe it was because he was so close it offered them the opportunity to build a special relationship and bond with him. They always had special presents for him and he even had his own room at their house. They took him out for special trips to the mall, and they stopped at the same restaurant and bought him food and sundaes like they did for me and Emily when we were small. They took him to many football, basketball, and baseball games, and they would buy the best tickets. They never did anything like that for Emily's children.

Watching my parents' relationship with Reese made me realize they had always favored me over Emily. I had never thought of that prospect before, but now it made sense. I was the one they'd bought Mr. Fur for, and I chose her name. Emily just agreed with me. I was the one that got a jewelry box full of beautiful jewelry and perfume after getting into Emily's things and spilling perfume everywhere. I was the one who ran off to college with no life goals, and they paid for it. Emily had gotten a scholarship. I was the one who took off jetting across the country, and I sent nothing but a few postcards. Then I had gotten married without a word to anybody.

Emily had always done everything right. She always made good grades in school, chose a career path upon entering college, went to law school, became a lawyer, married a lawyer, and planned her children's births. Reese hadn't been planned but was the product of our love at a perfect moment. I always believed he had been given to us by God. This epiphany made me feel bad for Emily. I had been pampered as I dawdled and twisted through life, and she did everything right. I had spent many years feeling sorry for myself and shutting the world off when really, the world was mine, and Emily had to work hard for everything she got in life. My parents spoiled Reese as much as they had spoiled me.

We wanted to enrich Reese's life and teach him about the world, so we took him many, many places. We went to amusement parks and rode roller coasters until we were ready to fall down. We raced go-carts. Reese was really good! When he was little he wanted to be a race car driver. So we took him to the races. He loved it! He would talk for hours about the fast cars and their loud engines. He wanted a car like they had, and he wanted it to go really fast. We took him to monster truck shows and he loved watching the trucks run over cars and other objects. We took him to football and baseball games. We even took him to professional wrestling matches. During the summers at home we barbecued, and we swam in our pool. Reese's friend Vince would come over and we ended up putting in a curvy slide. They loved the slide and would sometimes spend hot summer days pushing each other down the slide and sliding down it in odd positions.

Our favorite place to go though was the cabin. It was an escape from everything. When we were there in the winter we went sledding, pelted each other with snowballs, built snow families, and simply enjoyed being together. In the summer we went fishing in the creek, and we had bonfires where we'd make s'mores, and Cobie told him crazy, spooky ghost stories. We would look at the stars and Cobie would point out the constellations to Reese. In the spring and fall we fished, hiked, and camped. At Christmas Cobie and Reese would string up Christmas lights across the house. Every year our house became brighter. We had bought dirt bikes, and we'd go tear up the trails outside of town. Our lives were never dull, and Reese learned about the world.

Reese had transformed me. He made me face life head-on and put my own fear and insecurities behind me. He was my precious child and responsibility in life. He was the reason I was placed here on this earth. Before him and before Cobie, my life was empty. I stumbled aimlessly with no direction or reason to be. The man in the park—who I now believe wasn't a person at all, but a vision or maybe an angel—sent me on the path to finding Cobie. Cobie had been just as lost and confused as I was before we found each other. Finding each other gave us a purpose. That purpose was Reese. We had to see to it that he was safe and taken care of before we could care for ourselves. We had to be there for him and guide him through the process of growing up. We did this together as a family, and our love grew stronger. Cobie and I both had finally grown up ourselves.

The elderly lady reached her hand across the table as if she was holding onto something or someone, but nobody was there. She continued to rock and watch outside as the stars in the sky twinkled off the fresh snow.

Nikki

Sammy and Clay had a baby girl about two years after Reese was born. She was a breathtaking child with a full head of thick, luscious brown hair. Her eyes changed color, depending on her mood. Usually they were brown but when she was scared or upset, they turned green. Her name was Nicole, or Nikki for short. She loved Reese like a brother, and he loved her back. He was always there for her, watching over her, and protecting her from anything harmful in life. When they were young, he let her play with his cars and tools. He would fix her dolls when their legs, heads, and arms came off. She was like a little sister to him. When they were little they had their own language that nobody else could understand. As they grew older that language continued and blossomed. It was their secret code. Many times I wondered what they were saying. I wondered if Emily and I had a secret language as well. Something only siblings could understand. In school Reese watched out for her closely, and nobody ever messed with Nikki. I think they were afraid to. Being two years older than Nikki, he must have seemed large and frightening to the children her age. When anybody looked at her wrong, he stared back at them, giving them the evil eye.

Once at the mall a little boy ran up to Nikki and flipped her hair. Reese tripped the boy as he ran off. The boy ended up falling flat on his face. He then got up, started crying, and ran off. Reese wasn't a bully but he wouldn't allow anyone to harm Nikki in any way. He was like her guardian angel. As they grew older he would walk her home from school, and then he walked to the shop, or she would come with him to the shop. At the shop she was most impressed with his abilities. She would sit and watch mesmerized. He taught her how to check and change the oil in a car, how to check the tires for air and wear, and even how to change tires. He even taught her how to tune up a car.

She was like his little shadow. She loved his bug collection, and she wasn't afraid to hold the bugs. She was the only girl he would allow to go up in his bug sanctuary. They had a very special relationship.

Nikki grew up to be a very striking young lady, but Reese didn't seem to notice. I am not sure how, as she was always at his side. I guess he just hadn't thought of her in that way. She was more like the sibling he never had. As I watched them together, I couldn't help but compare their relationship to that of Cobie and me. I hadn't known Cobie my entire life, nor was I his shadow. But I was the young lady who did my best to be noticed by him. Sometimes he would notice me and sometimes not.

Reese, like his father at the same age, didn't seem overly interested in any young lady. Sometimes he paid them attention, took them out on dates, but then he never seemed to call them back. They always called him back, and he was usually too preoccupied to talk. I noticed many young ladies who vied for his attention but they didn't get it. Nikki had a lot of his attention, and she became very flirty with him as she entered high school and started to really notice boys. Boys noticed her too, but I think they were afraid to ask her out. Sometimes I would see her flirting with boys, but when Reese came around, the boys would leave. I think they feared him, and I wouldn't be surprised if they had good reason. I am sure he threatened one or two over the years. He didn't want Nikki to be a notch in any boy's belt. Nikki and Reese became especially close and spent an awful lot of time together the older they got.

In Reese's senior year he came to me and his father with a proposal. He wanted to help run the business and eventually take it over. We admired his dream, but both of us knew it took more than mechanical knowledge to keep it running smoothly and make money. We counteroffered, and told him he had to go to college to learn the business and financial part of owning a business. He wasn't too pleased at first. He really didn't like school. He was very intelligent, but he didn't seem to have time for school. He finally agreed to it. His dream was to take over the shop and expand it. He had tried to get me and his father to expand, but we weren't interested in the added responsibilities. We were pleased with our lives and the financial rewards we made from the shop.

When he went off to college Nikki became very lonely. Sometimes she would come by the shop, sit in her spot, and talk with us. She hung around so much that I decided I needed to keep her busy. I started showing her what I did in the office. She caught on very quickly, and she was extremely efficient. I offered her a part-time job working as my assistant. She was always asking about Reese and when he would be visiting next. Sometimes we took her with us when we would visit Reese. She enjoyed this, and he would show her around the campus and take her out around the town. He had always been her hero, her knight in shining armor.

At home, Nikki started getting more attention from boys without Reese around, and she found boyfriends. She loved the attention they gave her. After several very short relationships, she found a boy she really liked. He was an attractive-looking young man who was always giving her gifts. He treated her like a princess and put her on a pedestal high in heaven above. She seemed to absorb the attention from him like a sponge. Her parents really liked him as well. He was always polite and respectful, and he appeared to be without flaw. With her newfound admirer she seemed to forget about Reese somewhat. She didn't stop talking about him completely, but she spoke of him less than before.

Nikki and this boy dated for several months until one dreadful night. They had gone out on a date. He had made reservations at an exclusive restaurant. He bent over backward to impress her with romance. I think that is why she dated him so long. She loved the feeling of being at the center of his world and having his full attention. Nikki didn't come home that night and her parents were worried sick. Sammy called me, crying on the phone. I went over to their house and comforted her. We called the police and made a report. The police didn't seem to think it was any big deal that they weren't home and it was three in the morning. Nikki had always been very cautious with her curfew, and she was a good girl. I stayed with Sammy, Clay and Cobie went searching for them. First, they went by the boy's house, but he wasn't home either. Next they searched the area. They looked everywhere they could think to look, but they came back empty-handed.

Finally, the phone rang. We all jumped to get it. Reese was on the phone. Nikki had called him, and he had picked her up and was bringing her home. When they arrived at the house, Nikki seemed shaken up, but Reese was calm, although I could tell he was very angry about something. I could hear it in his voice. After dinner the boy had wanted to take her to a hotel, and she refused. He became very angry and forced himself on her. When he was finished, he yanked her out of the car. He told her that she was a "tease."

Crying and hysterical, she called Reese. He came to her rescue, and he sat with her, allowing her to tell him the whole story. When she was calm, he called and brought her home. After that night, Reese seemed to think of Nikki differently. She wasn't just his little shadow anymore but a young woman. He suddenly realized that she was a beautiful, precious, and blossoming young woman.

Nikki and Reese's relationship seemed to heighten. He came home more frequently to visit. He didn't come to visit us though. He came to visit Nikki. I loved Nikki but it was difficult for me to take a backseat to her. Cobie seemed amused by it and encouraged it. Sometimes I got so upset at Cobie for encouraging it I would start a fight. I knew I was being silly and insane, but I wasn't ready to lose my little boy. I also knew I had probably sent mixed messages over the years. I had often compared their relationship to mine and Cobie's, and I had encouraged their friendship; it was different now. He was finally really noticing her and taking a huge interest. I had to realize my baby boy was growing up and making his own life path. He was following the journey where his heart was leading him.

Over the summers he always came home and worked in the shop. We started showing him more about the business, and he offered us new ideas. Nikki also still worked in the shop part time. I watched their relationship change right before my eyes the summer before Nikki went to college. They would laugh and play flirtatiously in the shop, go to lunch together, and lose track of time. He now paid more attention to her than he did engines, transmissions, and drivetrains. Watching them together made it easier for me to let go of Reese. He was now a man and not a boy.

In the fall, Reese went back to school and Nikki went to college. She insisted on going to the same school as Reese, and Reese wanted that as well. They didn't come home and visit as much. We had to visit them. They were in their own lovers' world, and we were just parents. They came home over the summer, and they announced to us they were getting married after Reese graduated the following spring. I wasn't sure then what Nikki's plans were for school. I think the only reason she went to school was to please her parents and to be close to Reese. I think her plans were to quit school altogether, knowing that she and Reese could not only successfully run the business but expand on it. Sammy and Clay were elated with Nikki and Reese's engagement. They always loved Reese like we loved Nikki. Who would have thought when Sammy and I were children and best friends that our children would marry each other one day? That night we celebrated. We all went out for dinner, had a huge feast, and toasted our children's engagement.

For the next year Sammy worked with Nikki to plan the wedding. I think Sammy did more planning than Nikki. She was so excited, and she wanted this wedding perfect for her daughter. Nikki loved the beach. Her dream in life was to live in a house that overlooked the beach. She wanted to be able to open her windows and hear the sound of the waves gently pounding the shore. So Sammy planned a wedding on the beach. The wedding turned out to be breathtaking. There were many vibrantly colorful tropical flowers everywhere. Reese looked very handsome. He reminded me so much of his father.

The memories of Cobie and me twenty some years ago came flooding back. I clearly remembered the night in Vegas when he asked me to marry him, and then folded and slipped a $100 dollar bill on my finger. I still wore that ring just beside my wedding ring he later bought. Looking out at the beach and hearing the sound of the surf brought back memories of us traveling the world and holding each other on the beach as the surf rolled in over us.

I could feel the tears welling up in my eyes as I looked at my grown son. I gave him a hug but couldn't get any words out of my mouth except, "I love you." He whispered back, "I love you too, Mom." I held him for the last time as my boy. Cobie came over and we held each other. I knew he felt it too. Our child was grown, and he was about to be married. Nikki looked stunning. She was so beautiful it was enough to knock any man off his feet. I could see Reese looking at her the same way Cobie had always looked at me. I knew this was right for them. I did my best to hold back my tears during the wedding.

After the wedding I stole off and sat down in the sand. I watched the tide roll in and out and cried. My entire life was passing before my eyes. After a while, Cobie found me, sat down in the sand beside me, and grabbed my hand. We sat there together, holding hands until we could see the sun just starting to set, and then we walked back. The reception was held right on the beach. There was music, and everybody was dancing and drinking champagne. I felt ready to join in the celebration. For their wedding gift we had purchased two round-trip tickets to Hawaii, rented them a condo on the beach, and given them a key to the cabin.

The elderly lady continued to rock and she now closed her eyes. Outside the snow appeared silver gray as the stars began to fade and the moon went into hiding.

Renew

With Nikki and Reese around we spent less and less time at the shop. We weren't needed, and we knew they wanted to do this on their own. We started spending more time with each other. At first we spent days, and then we spent weeks at the cabin. It was like we were getting to know each other over again. The cabin was so peaceful and serene. It was like having a slice of heaven. Every morning Cobie and I went for a walk. He would find the most beautiful flowers, place them in a vase, and set them directly in the center of the table. I would always keep each day's flowers and place the petals in a dish in the bathroom. At night we sat outside under the stars, counting each one and admiring their beauty. Each star had its own unique qualities, like how often and how brightly it would twinkle. When it was cold we sat inside on the twin rockers, we rocked holding hands or holding each other in front of the fire, watching the stars at night. We reminisced about our lives together.

When we were home we helped take care of our parents who were becoming quite elderly. We ran errands for them and helped them cook, clean, and take care of their yards. Sometimes we just spent time watching movies and chatting with them. Cobie's mother wasn't getting around much, and his father was very hard of hearing. My parents were still in good health, but they didn't have the energy they once did. We did our best to help them out, and we spent some time checking on Nikki and Reese, but they always had things completely under control.

For our twenty-fifth anniversary, Cobie bought me a dazzling silver convertible sports car. The car was gorgeous and fully loaded with a leather interior. I had never had my own vehicle. I usually drove the work truck, or when we were together as a family we rode in Cobie's truck, and he drove. I was speechless. He handed me the keys, we got in, and I drove. We weren't driving to any special destination. We were simply driving. We had the top down, the radio blaring, and we drove. I felt like a sixteen-year-old driving my first car. This car shifted so smoothly and ran so quietly. I wasn't sure sometimes if it was still running.

I got on the freeway, and I headed out of town. I didn't know what I could get him that would even compare to the gift he had given me, but as we drove I kept thinking. We drove all night, singing and talking like two teenagers. Eventually Cobie fell asleep, and I was on my own. As I drove I noticed a sign that said Las Vegas. I followed the signs and continued on to Las Vegas. What better gift could I give him than to go back to where we found each other?

The sun was starting to come up as we entered Las Vegas and Cobie woke up. He looked around. It took him a minute or two to register where we were. Once he figured it out, he smiled at me with his cute dimple, laughed, and he said I was insane. I laughed too. I remember that day when he had to lock me in the truck to show me I was rich. I had calmed down since then, and I wasn't quite so fiery. We drove through the city until I found the hotel where we gambled. I pulled up in valet parking. They took the keys, I handed them a twenty-dollar bill, and we headed inside. It looked pretty much the same as I remembered it. I had been quite drunk and out of sorts that night, but nothing really stuck out as different.

This was my present and my venture. Cobie had always surprised me with something, and now it was my turn. I checked us in, making sure we had a room with a hot tub. The room was incredible. We had a fully stocked refrigerator and bar, and a view of the entire city from our window. I was too tired from driving all night to enjoy the view or do anything but sleep. Cobie closed the windows, and we lay down. I went to sleep immediately, wrapped in his arms. I could feel him breathing, and I could smell him. I had always loved the way he smelled. That was the last thing I remembered before I fell asleep. I woke up to Cobie caressing my hair, my face, and then my neck. He started kissing me softly and whispered in my ear that I was as beautiful now as the day we met. I met his kisses with mine and we held each other closely as we shared our love for each other. Eventually we made it downstairs to the casino, but the evening was still young. We went for a walk, stopped, and ate dinner.

After dinner we stopped in one of the casinos, gambled a little, and had a few drinks. We didn't win anything and left. We walked to the little chapel we had been married in. It still had the same name and the open twenty-four hours sign flashing out front. We went inside. It was decorated differently, but otherwise it was the same. Different people worked there, and they asked again if they could help us. They saw my ring, and they asked if we wanted to renew our vows. It was just like twenty-five years ago. I smiled at Cobie, and he asked me to step outside with him. I did. Outside he asked for my left hand. I gave him my hand, and he tenderly slipped off my wedding ring and my folded $100 bill. Then he slipped the $100 bill back on my finger, and asked me to marry him for a third time. I hugged him, and answered yes. We went back inside, and were married for a third time.

After the wedding, we told them our story about how we had been married here twenty-five years ago. They congratulated us on our twenty-five years, and they asked if they could take a photo of us. They kept an album of couples like us who had lasted and had come back a second time. We allowed them to take the picture, and they placed it into their album. We also received a copy of it. I kept it in our wedding album, and I wrote twenty-five years on the back.

We were the only people besides those at the chapel that knew our true anniversary. It had always been our little secret and we would swap small gifts on this day. After we were remarried, we strolled back to the hotel and casino, and we gambled the rest of the night away. Once again I had too many drinks, and I became very tipsy. I'm not sure what it was about this city, but it seemed to be the only place I drank alcohol. I didn't black out though, and I remember the night clearly. We had started out on a losing streak before we were remarried, but we ended up on a winning streak after we were remarried. We went directly to the tables. I didn't remember the last time and didn't know my secret to winning, but as I played I saw the numerical patterns. The patterns and numbers would flash through my head, and again we won thousands. After a few hours at the tables we took our winnings and retired to our room and hot tub. The warm, bubbly water felt good against my body. The next day we headed home.

When we arrived home I noticed a note stuck to our door. It was from Nikki. She asked us to call when we got home. I wasted no time in calling. She sounded very excited, and she asked if we could come over for dinner about six. She said they had something exciting to tell us. I assumed it had to do with the business. They never kept us out of the loop, and they told us everything they were doing. Already

Reese had expanded the garage to include a full body shop, and he had purchased another shop in our local area. He was making his dream come true. He had seen potential in the business we hadn't been motivated enough to see.

Late that afternoon Cobie's father called. I saw Cobie's face turn white as a sheet. He dropped the phone, and he rushed me out the door. He didn't say what had happened or where we were going, but my stomach told me it wasn't good. Something truly wrong had happened. We ended up at the hospital. Cobie's mother was very ill, and the doctors didn't know if she was going to make it. Cobie's father was sitting beside his wife, holding her hand, and telling her everything was going to be OK. The next few days were rough. Her condition was touch and go and getting worse. She asked for Cobie. He went to her bedside and sat with her. She told him how much she loved her boys, Cobie, his father, and Reese. Then she asked for him to take her home. She knew it was the end, and she wanted to die in her home with her family. He complied with her wishes and took her home. We all stayed with her for her final hours. I didn't find out until several weeks later what Nikki's big surprise was.

Cobie's father became very depressed and sullen when he lost his wife. We spent a lot of time with him, taking care of him, but he seemed to have given up. Cobie had a very difficult time dealing with his mother's death as well. He was an only child. His parents had planned on having a large family, but after Cobie was born his mother was unable to have any more children. She had loved him with all her heart, and she had cherished him dearly.

Nikki and Reese weren't just worried about Grandpa, they were worried about us. They brought us all over dinner one night, and they finally spilled their news. They had been as preoccupied and sullen as everyone else with Grandma's death, and they hadn't felt the timing was right. Now they felt the timing was perfect. How better to mourn someone's life that you loved than to bring a new life into the world. Nikki was pregnant, and they were about to have Grandpa's first great-grandbaby. When they told us the news, Cobie's father cried with joy. This great-grandbaby gave him a reason to live. He had to stick around for this baby to be born. Nikki insisted the baby was a girl, and she wanted to name her Natalie after her recently deceased great-grandmother. Cobie's father lived long enough to see and hold his great-grandbaby, Natalie. He died just hours after he held her.

Natalie was the most precious baby girl. She looked identical to me. I knew Reese had my genes somewhere in him, but I could never find them. Now I had found them, as he passed them on to his child. Natalie had a way of wrapping everyone around her finger. When she smiled and laughed the entire world seemed to get brighter, and when she cried the world would grow darker. She was the master of the days, the moon, and the clouds in the sky. The world seemed to revolve around her. She looked at the world through her deep blue baby eyes, and she seemed in awe of what she saw. She always had her tiny little fists balled up as if she was holding onto some little secret. Cobie and I spent a lot of time with Natalie. Nikki mostly worked out of the house now, but we stayed with Natalie on the days Nikki had to go to work. Many times we brought her over to visit with my parents. They adored their beautiful great-grandbaby, and they would talk about how much she looked and acted like me. When she smiled, laughed, and cooed to my parents it was like they flew back in time and I was a baby again.

Losing both his parents in less than a year's time was difficult on Cobie, but Natalie seemed to fill the void in his heart. He loved her every bit as much as he loved Reese. Reese was thrilled with her. She was his little angel, and she was too perfect but to have come from anywhere but heaven. Nikki was a very protective mother. That is why she mostly worked from home now. She felt that a garage full of mechanics was an inappropriate place to raise a little girl. Reese agreed. It had been OK for him when he was a baby, but it wasn't right for their little girl. Sammy was elated over her grandbaby, and as dueling grandparents either we had to schedule our time with Natalie or share it together. We chose many times to share it, taking Natalie many places. We took her to the mall, and we would come home with bags of goodies for her. She was the best dressed baby on the Pacific Coast. We also took her to fashion shows. We even took her to the symphony. I had never had a little girl to do these activities with, but Sammy had, and with her experience we showed Natalie the feminine world.

The day we took Natalie to the symphony I was reunited with a friend from the past. My clarinet-playing roommate, Tia, had accomplished her dream, and her music was just as magical as it had been years ago when I would listen to her play. After the symphony we had dinner, and I told Sammy and Natalie all about her and how I would spend hours listening to her play, mesmerized by the music that she would make. It had amazed me that blowing into a piece of metal could produce such beautiful sounds and caress every sense within the human body.

The next day I looked her up, and I found her phone number and address. I gave her a call, and we met for lunch. We shared our lives with each other. She told me about her life in music. She and her boyfriend had wed after graduation, but they were soon divorced. She was married to her career, and he couldn't accept being second in her life. She had never gotten remarried, and had taken back her maiden name. She had played for various symphonies, and had given private lessons to young, aspiring students.

I told her about my nightmare job after college, how I had taken off wandering around the country, and about Cobie. She was impressed with my life, and she said she admired me. I had found my true love. She had spent so many years trying to make it to the top that she didn't have anyone or anything but her music. She envied me that I didn't have to go home alone; I had a husband, a child, and a grandchild to share my life with. She felt her life was empty now, and she wished she had spent more time enjoying life.

As she spoke I began to think about what my life may have been like if Nathan hadn't disappeared. If we had gotten married, would we have ended up like Tia and her husband, divorced after only a couple of years? He was a military man, and I wanted to be an actress. Acting takes dedication and determination. No famous star did "nothing" to get a career off the ground. Actors had to work to get where they were. Nathan was a military man, and we would have been traveling the world, living here and there. I never would have been able to follow my dreams if I had married him. I would have had two options: one, to settle down, forget my dreams, and be a wife; or two, divorce him to follow my dreams. This realization had never struck me before. Nathan and I were never meant to be married. It would have never worked. I would have been traveling the world over because I had no choice, not because I wanted to. If I'd had to give up my career dreams, I would have spent my life resenting Nathan. If I had left Nathan, I would have spent my life wondering like Tia, what if? I was happy with my life that I had chosen, and that I didn't follow my dreams because they had died with Nathan. I had never thought of it as captivating as Tia seemed to find it. It was simply my life, and I lived it to the fullest of my abilities. I loved Cobie, and I had never given my life with him a second look.

When I got home later that afternoon, I compulsively went up into our attic. I had never been up in the attic in all the years we had lived in this house but my past life was up there, and I now suddenly had questions that I needed answered — questions that I had never been curious about before, questions I had always thought were better left unanswered. I didn't even know what I was looking for, but I somehow thought I would find it in my attic. When Cobie and I had gotten married and bought our house, I had him place all my belongings from my parents' house, my childhood, in the attic. Along with those items were the boxes I had had from my college life and life on my own before my journey. When I had moved out of my apartment, I had everything sent to my parents' house. Now it was time to rediscover my life and find my answers.

I easily found my boxes. I looked at the labels on the boxes. They were all taped. I pulled the tape away from the ones from my childhood. I slowly looked through them, and I found pictures, clothing, and items that had memories like my jewelry box and some stuffed animals. Then I found a small box inside one of the larger boxes. It was full of letters and the roses Nathan had sent me that I had dried. The letters were all from Nathan. I read all of the letters and studied them, not knowing what I was going to find. In the letters before the war, he mostly wrote about the military and the men he served with. In the few letters I received from Nathan after the war, he wrote mostly about me and wanting to see me again.

He wrote a little about his life at war but not much. He kept mentioning a man he called Turtle. I am not sure why he called him Turtle, but they had become friends in boot camp. Turtle was an important piece to this puzzle. There were a few unopened letters that my parents must have received after I left. The glue on the letters was dried and brittle from sitting in our attic all those years. I opened them up, and in them he talked about being wounded and losing his arm. Not only was he wounded, but Turtle had been wounded at the same time. He kept talking about how my letters gave him strength, how he kept my picture close to his heart, and looked at it daily. He talked about his excitement in coming home, and how he couldn't wait to see me again. None of this made any sense to my brain. I just couldn't register what happened. I had always assumed he had left me. He hadn't left me, but somehow he had never made it home. I stared at the letters in disbelief with tears falling down my cheeks. What had happened to Nathan? Had I been the one to leave him?

After several minutes of crying, I spied a package. The package, unopened, was from Nathan's father, but the address wasn't their address here. It was sent from Texas a little over five years after Nathan had disappeared. I picked it up, and I could feel a box inside it. I didn't want to open it out of my own guilt. I took the package, held it to my chest, and cried. I cried for a love that had been lost to the war. The war had somehow torn us apart. I finally opened the package. Inside I could feel the box, and I pulled it out. The box said "Purple Heart." I knew the Purple Heart was given to military personal injured in the line of duty. Why had Nathan's father sent me his Purple Heart? I opened up the box, and inside was this prestigious medal that Nathan's father had sent to me. Now I seemed to have more questions than ever. What had happened to Nathan, and why did I have this medal? This medal belonged to Nathan, to his family. I didn't deserve this medal. I thought the worst of Nathan. My heart wanted to believe that he had left me, but he hadn't left me. He had loved me. I had left him. Like a ghost, I silently went downstairs and sat on the couch. I held the box in front of me, and I tried to make sense in my head about why I had this Purple Heart in my possession.

As I sat on the couch staring at the box, I heard the key in the door and Cobie enter. He was talking about spending the afternoon with Reese, Nikki, and our grandchild. He walked over to me, asking about my lunch with Tia. I didn't answer. He seemed so far away, like he was in an alternate universe trying to reach me. He sat on the couch beside me, and he was silent. I had been so focused on finding answers when I had gotten home that I had been oblivious to the fact that I was alone. I hadn't thought once about Cobie since I had gotten home. I had been entangled in my own web, searching for answers.

We both sat silently on the couch for some time when Cobie finally spoke. He spoke in circles, and he didn't seem sure of what he was saying or how to say it. After he rambled for a few minutes I handed him the box, and I asked him to open it. He took the box and opened it. When he was able to get control of his words, he told me how it was thought that Nathan had been taken a prisoner of war. How could Cobie know this? He and Nathan weren't friends. With tears still rolling down my cheeks, I asked him how he knew this. He said that when he had worked as a handyman, one of the men he worked with had been in the war. He and this man had become friends. He told him war stories, and he talked about Nathan and the other men who had been in battle with him. Nathan had been in a helicopter headed home when it was shot down by enemy fire. All of the bodies but Nathan's had been recovered. They were badly burned, but their dog tags didn't lie. It was then assumed that Nathan had been found by the enemy and taken prisoner. There seemed to be more that he wanted to say, but he stopped speaking and became very silent again. Why, after all these years that we had been married, did he never tell me any of this? I suddenly felt infuriated, and my face seemed to turn a fire-engine red. I didn't even know what to say to him. Then I got up and went for a walk. I had to reconcile the day's events in my mind.

Nathan had never left me. I had given him strength and courage to fight in the war. My place in his life had been one of grave importance, and that was why his father had given me his Purple Heart. Nathan and I were never meant to be married; like Tia's, our marriage probably never would have worked. I then thought of Cobie and our life together. We were meant to be together. Our life together was full and complete. He was the man God had intended me to be with, and the fact that Cobie hadn't told me any of this before didn't matter. Maybe he had been trying to protect me, or he just didn't know how to tell me; whatever the reason, it didn't matter. My heart belonged to Cobie and my family. I walked home to Cobie where he sat on our front patio waiting for me. I walked up to him, held him, and never spoke another word about Nathan. Cobie placed Nathan's Purple Heart on our mantel where it stayed.

My parents were growing very old and weren't able to take care of themselves anymore. For years we had gone over to their house and helped them out, but it wasn't enough anymore. We decided to bring them to our house, so we could take care of them and make their final days as comfortable and filled with love as possible. We catered to their every need. They loved to reminisce over Emily and me when we were little. The stories they told we had heard hundreds of times, but we didn't stop them from telling them all over again. Telling these stories made their eyes twinkle and they would laugh.

Reese and Nikki came over as much as possible. My mother loved to hold Nikki's hand. Sometimes they would just sit silently, and other times my mother would talk about me. She told Nikki everything about my childhood and young adult life. She would be very serious and not just reminiscing while telling her stories. Nikki listened intently, and she seemed to be in deep thought trying to find the meaning of what my mother was trying to tell her. I knew what my mother was telling her. She was telling her all about me, and she was offering insight about her own daughter, Natalie.

My mother's mind was still very lucid. My father though was becoming more and more forgetful. He mostly sat quietly and watched his great-granddaughter as she learned to crawl and form sounds. Sometimes he would watch his favorite TV shows. He died sitting quietly watching TV. My mother's mind seemed to go after my father died. She would sit and talk to him as if he was there, and she would reach over to hold his hand but nobody was there. I wondered if he was actually there in some spirit form, telling her it was time to go; time to go to heaven.

One night I bolted awake out of my dream, which I have never been able to remember, and I rushed to my mother's room. She was sleeping soundly. I gently sat down beside her, and I placed my hand in hers. She softly squeezed my hand, and I felt a rush of energy pulse through my veins. Every memory of my parents worked its way through my brain from present to birth. Her grip loosened and her breathing stopped. I laid my head down on her chest and wept softly.

My parents didn't live to see their second great-grandbaby born, Jacob Samuel. For the four lives that God had taken to heaven he gave us two new ones.

The elderly woman no longer rocked gently but steadily in her chair. But from time to time she would give the chair a tender push. Her eyes remained closed. The moon and stars had completely vanished, and the sun was beginning to stretch its lazy arms.

Old Friends

Natalie was a very insightful and inquisitive child. She was also precocious, adventurous, and spunky. As she grew older, it was like looking in a mirror and seeing me. She had my wavy golden hair and bright green mysterious eyes. When she became upset she simply curled up, pulled her quilt over her, and fell asleep. She loved to get into my jewelry and perfume. I couldn't get upset. I remembered how in awe I had been over Emily's pretty trinkets and wonderful-smelling perfumes. I gave Natalie my old jewelry box and filled it with costume jewelry, little perfumes, and lip glosses. She insisted that it stay on my dresser next to mine. Sometimes together we would go into my bedroom, place our jewelry on each other, and make up our faces and hair.

We had a very special bond, and we were like two kindred spirits. I knew her every thought because I could feel it.

I shared with her all the stories of my life. She was the only person who could appreciate and completely understand me. I told her about how her other grandmother and I were best friends growing up, about the shape-shifters. I told her about my depression, the man in the park, and how I had traveled the country in search of the light at the end of my tunnel. I told her how her grandfather and I found each other. He had been the strong arms that pulled me from the pit of my own darkness. I told her about my trip to Vegas and the money we had made. About how her grandfather locked me in a truck, how we got married in Vegas, and how she was the only person besides us who knew our real anniversary.

I told Natalie everything about my life except my time spent with Nathan. It seemed irrelevant to talk about that chapter in my life when I had such a wonderful and beautiful family. I had always assumed that Nathan had left me, but maybe in my heart I knew that he had died. It had always been easier for my fragile heart to accept that he left me. Somehow I didn't know if it really mattered anymore. I had found my one true love, and our love had created our beautiful family.

I told her stories about her parents growing up and about her great-grandparents that she barely remembered. I told her about my grandparents. She would listen quietly, and I knew the wheels in her head were spinning rapidly as she soaked up everything I said.

Jacob was the perfect combination of both his parents. He had his father's smile, curiosity for bugs, and hair, but his mother's eyes and temperament. He was very busy, and he loved Natalie very much. He followed Natalie everywhere and wanted to do everything she did. She loved her younger brother, and she would push him on the swing in their backyard and help him find bugs. Cobie fixed up the tree house in our backyard for Jacob. Natalie had insisted on helping. When they were finished it was better than before. Sometimes they would spend hours in the tree house. Nobody really knew what all they did up there, but it was their private magical kingdom in the sky.

After Natalie started school, Reese began taking Jacob to work with him. Nikki didn't exactly like the idea, but Jacob was lonely at home so she didn't argue. Jacob loved to be with his father, and they had a very special relationship, but he wasn't interested in cars and what made them work. He was interested in why the sun came out during the day, and why the moon and stars shone brilliantly at night. He wanted to know how fish could live in the seas and birds in the air. He loved the cabin, being high above the earth in the clouds.

Cobie and I grew even closer after the births of our grandchildren. I had thought we were as close as two people could be but we became like one entire person. We spent as much time as we could with our son, Nikki, and our grandchildren, but we spent a lot of time just the two of us. We spent time at the cabin, and we picked up where we had left off traveling the world, seeing all the sights that were left to see. We took long, leisurely cruises, and we traveled the country retracing our steps before we were married. I showed him Frank's Pizza House where we stopped and ate pizza. I showed him my first apartment and where I worked. We visited the beach where I had gotten stuck in the hurricane and the motel where I had stayed. He showed me the mountains where he lived working odd jobs. He showed me the many places he had worked as a plumber and handyman, and how he had found the perfect spot for the cabin and had it built for us.

I hadn't known in all these years that he had it built. I always thought he had found it and purchased it. Evidently he had found the spot while hiking in the mountains. He had come to the mountain to camp alone for a few weeks, and he had wandered off a trail. He enjoyed the mountain air and silence. It was a place he said helped clear his head. He hiked to the top to look out over the valley. This was the spot, his spot, where he later had the cabin built.

In our travels we also visited Emily. Emily's husband had died a few years ago, and now it was just her and occasionally Trey. The kids were grown and she hadn't any grandchildren yet. Tansey had become an attorney like her parents. She was a defense attorney, and Trent had gone to a military college and was now an officer and pilot. He had liked military school so well that he didn't want to give it up. These career choices seemed fitting for T and T. Like me, Trey didn't have any career path or goals for his life after high school. Emily had talked him into going to college, and he had spent four years getting a two-year degree. Recently he had been in touch with Reese. He had always admired Reese, and he wanted to help him out with the shop. I thought it sounded like a wonderful idea, but it wasn't my decision. It was great to see my sister and know that T and T hadn't become criminals in need of their parents' legal services; instead, they had found positive ways to assert their evil energy.

At home, Sammy called early one morning, excited with news to share with me. Sarah had called her, and she was going to be in town for the weekend. I hadn't seen Sarah since high school, but I had heard about her life through Sammy. Sarah had stayed in town after Sammy and I left for college. She worked in her mother's antique shop. Mark, the boy who stood up to Boogie Woman, had gone to war, and when he returned home he and Sarah hit it off and later became married. He had stayed in the military, and they had traveled and lived all over the world.

It made me sad to remember how I had abandoned my friends. They had been my best friends. We had been like superglue. Sammy didn't think it was any big deal, and she was sure that Sarah would love to see me. I was excited to see Sarah, but I was a little resistant as well. Cobie thought it was a great idea, and he convinced me I should see her. Late Friday evening Sarah arrived at Sammy's house. I wasn't sure what to expect. I deserved a slap on my face, and I felt that I owed her an explanation. She welcomed me though with open arms, and she didn't ask for any explanation of my past actions. I thought I owed it, and I offered her an apology and an explanation. She smiled and told me I had always been weird that way. She had never been able to figure out what had been going through my head, and why I behaved in the ways that I did, but that was what she had loved about me when we were kids. She said I was "passionate, unpredictable, and lived in an alternate reality." What she said made me take a good look at myself. She was right. My views of life were always skewed compared to others, and I heightened events in my life into my mind's drama. Cobie had always told me I was fiery, crazy, and spirited. That is why he had fallen in love with me.

Sammy, Sarah, and I spent what was left of the evening sharing our lives with each other. I learned that Sarah and Mark had three children. The oldest, a son, had joined the military like his father. He was married, and they had three children, two boys and one girl. Their daughter had joined the FBI, and she was married with two children, a boy and a girl. The youngest child was another boy, and he had wild dreams of becoming an actor on the big screen. He had moved to New York first and now he was living in southern California. He wasn't married, didn't have children, and was still chasing his dream. Sammy and I shared our lives as well. We told her about our children who had married each other, and we showed her pictures of our beautiful grandchildren, Natalie and Jacob.

Sarah explained to us how she and Mark had spent the last couple of years trying to track down all the people we had graduated with. She had even decided to track down Annabel. She told us the story of how she thought she had seen her on the cover of a magazine many years ago, but she was too busy being a mom to worry about it. She had bought the magazine and kept it. Recently she had found out who the model was on the cover of the magazine. She was known as Natasha. So Sarah proceeded to find out as much as she could about Natasha. She learned that Natasha had started out as a model, then filmed a couple of movies in Europe, and then she filmed in the United States. She had married a musician, divorced him, and married an actor. She then divorced him and married a songwriter who she stayed married to until his death eight years ago. He had been killed in a plane crash. After that Natasha disappeared. The rumor was that she died of a broken heart.

Sarah being stubborn kept poking until she found Natasha. She enlisted her daughter's help. She found that Natasha had died, at least figuratively speaking. She no longer went by Natasha, but the name Bell, and she lived in the mountains of North Carolina. Sarah felt she had gone this far, and had nothing to lose, so she called her. She wasn't home but she left her message stating who she was, left a number where she could be reached, and asked her to call back. Several weeks later Sarah received a phone call from Bell. She explained how Bell had seemed apprehensive at first. She wasn't sure why she called her, and she didn't know who she was or what she wanted. Sarah, being Sarah told her where she had grown up and gone to school. She explained to her how she was tracking down classmates, and how her picture had reminded her of a girl she had gone to school with. Sarah went on explain the entire conversation, but to make a long story short, Bell was Annabel, and she had dropped off the face of the earth for peace and quiet. Being a supermodel and an actress, she never had a moment's peace, so she moved to the mountains of North Carolina where she thought nobody would find her. She told us stories about our other classmates as well, but Annabel was the most exciting.

Mark and Sarah wanted to get all our graduating classmates together for a reunion here in town. She was asking Sammy and me to help. Sammy was the planner, not me. I had always done things spontaneously. I never knew what was going to happen next until it happened. I wasn't sure either if I really wanted to see everyone. I knew we had all changed, and we had grown up, but Sammy and Sarah were my best friends, and then Tony came along. I wondered about Tony, and where his life had taken him. I reflected on my own life, where it had taken me, and I decided to help plan the reunion.

Sarah went back home late Sunday evening and Monday morning Sammy was knocking on my door ready to start. We started by looking at the guest list, and we saw how many classmates Sarah had actually found. She had found 174 including the three of us. Next we started looking for a place to rent. Sammy insisted it not be elaborate but casual, as nobody our age wanted or should have to show up in a dress and heels. We found a convention center. She booked the entertainment, decided on the decorations, and she and Sarah worked out the catering details. Everything turned out beautiful.

The reunion was scheduled for a Saturday in the spring, and there was a really good turnout. Not everybody who was invited came. A few people were in failing health, and a few just didn't show, but it turned out to be a wonderful night. Sarah and Sammy were there early, making sure that everything was the way it was supposed to be. Cobie and I showed up late, as I wasn't in any hurry. When we entered, I barely recognized anyone at first. It had been so many years since I had seen these people. We walked around the room making small talk. Cobie didn't know anyone either. Suddenly a woman came up to me and just started talking like we were old friends. I listened to her talk and studied her face, trying to figure out who she was. I really didn't pay attention to what she was saying. It irritated me that I didn't know her, and I was very preoccupied with determining who she was. She was wearing a low-cut dress meant for someone half her age, and she had much too much makeup on and smelled like a perfume factory. Finally, I had it. She was Jennifer! I had never been friends with her; in fact, I couldn't stand her, but there she was talking to me. I politely continued my conversation with her, and I found out that she had become an editor for a tabloid, had been married and widowed twice to rich men, and had a step-daughter.

Cobie skipped out, leaving me alone with her. While she was rambling on about her life, which she thought was glamorous, I thought I spied Tony. I excused myself from her conversation, and I walked over to where I had seen Tony. He wasn't there anymore, but I saw Francisca, or at least it looked like Francisca, only plumper. I introduced myself to her and we began talking. It was nice to have a two-sided conversation with someone. It turned out that she had gotten married right after high school, and they had raised a large family. She had six children: two boys and four girls. She had never worked outside of her home. I guess raising six children, she didn't have time to work. She now had thirteen grandchildren and another on the way. Wow! I showed her my two grandchildren and she showed me her thirteen. Soon everybody was pulling out their pictures of children and grandchildren, and talking about their careers and lives.

Timothy had worked his way through medical school, and he became a surgeon. He had married and had two beautiful children, and now he had one grandchild.

Somehow Jennifer made her way over to us. I guess there was more of a crowd then around her. I left before she could speak to me, but she followed me. I couldn't get rid of her. It was like she was stalking me. She just kept rambling on and on. She told me about how Jules had married a rich man for his money, but with their extravagant lifestyle the money soon ran out. He went home to his parents, but they hated her, so she ended up homeless on the street, and she overdosed on drugs. Her body was found two days later. She went on about how horrible it had been that the driver was never found in Carry's accident. I also heard about Regina, who ended up pregnant out of wedlock her sophomore

year in college. He left her, and she was
forced to give the baby up for adoption.
She then rambled on about how Marco
had ended up a garbage man, Matthias
a dishwasher at an exclusive restaurant,
and Josh had become a bookie.

Finally, Sammy came over and
saved me from Jennifer's nonstop
ramblings. She brought me to Tony.
Tony was now bald on top. His wife,
Carla, was at least thirty years younger.
He had worked as a broker and later
sold real estate. He and his wife had a
ten-year-old child. I couldn't imagine
what it would be like to raise Reese at
my age. I loved my grandchildren, and I
spent a lot of time with them, but that
was different. I caught Cobie's glance,
and he and Clay came over and joined
us. Cobie was careful not to sit within
my arms' or legs' reach, as I was
infuriated. He had left me alone — with
Jennifer!

After a few minutes, Sarah and
Mark made their way over. We talked
for a while, watched everyone, and then
we saw her, Rebecca. After being
tormented by Jennifer, I decided

nothing could be worse. I walked over to Rebecca, introduced myself, and invited her to sit with us. She complied. It turned out that she had been the first female CEO of a very large and powerful corporation until the stress got to her. She retired and started writing children's books. The seven of us talked and reminisced about our lives for the remainder of the evening.

I decided I was glad that I had gone, and that Sarah had been so insistent on having the reunion. When I was a child I had considered school to be the first evil. As I grew older I knew that not to be true. I had never liked school though, and I didn't make any effort to keep in touch with anyone. It hadn't mattered to me what happened in their lives. I felt saddened by Jennifer. She couldn't accept that she had lost her youth and wasn't beautiful anymore. It was like her mind was stuck in high school but her body was stuck in the here and now. Her dress was so low cut that I could tell she had had implants. Looking at her aging face, I could tell she had had face lifts, eye lifts, and any other kind of lift, but she couldn't fight time and gravity. I felt bad for Regina, Jules, and Carry. They were so evil in school, and they treated people so horribly, it seemed they received their just desserts. Rebecca turned out OK. I'm not sure how, but I guess she had always had a heart, it was just muffled inside. Tony was a good guy, but I felt bad that he might never have the opportunity to see his son grow up fully and become a man. If he lives long enough to see him grow up, will he have a chance to see his grandchildren? Worse, will his grandchildren ever know him? Sarah, Sammy, and I had been very lucky. We had lived very fulfilling lives and had found love, happiness, and joy.

The elderly lady rocked no longer. She had fallen into a very deep sleep. The sky was still gray, as the sun hadn't appeared yet over the mountaintop.

Emily

Life had become lazy; we now spent most of our time at home embracing the languid days as each strolled by. Each one I preserved as if it was an artifact that could somehow transcend time. During the spring and summer evenings Cobie barbecued. We would sit on our patio underneath the stars, soaking in life around us. Since we had stopped working we had taken up gardening. We had a trellis covered in wisteria, and morning glories climbed the fences, opening up a brilliant blue in the morning and closing at night. It was as if they were talking, saying, *good morning and good night*. Miniature roses were planted along our patio. They had radiant blooms in yellows, golds, reds, pinks, and lavenders. We had plumbagos around our fence line; their flowers a delicate bluish lavender. We had randomly planted a wide assortment of small flowering trees with delightful fragrances. Around the pool we had planted geraniums in all colors. When in bloom they were a vibrant, eye-catching sight.

Sometimes we would share our evenings with Sammy, Clay, Reese, Nikki, Natalie, and Jacob. Sometimes it was just the two of us. I think I enjoyed the evenings when we were all together the most. Natalie and Jacob would run around the yard catching bugs, mostly moths. Jacob always wanted to catch a lightning bug, but we didn't have any. The only place I had ever seen them was on the East Coast. Cobie had given Jacob his great-grandmother's butterfly collection. He thought it was such a treasure, and he treated it like it was a precious gemstone. Natalie loved to dance around, doing cartwheels and round offs. Sometimes we would turn on the pool light and Natalie and Jacob would swim and hurtle themselves down the slide, challenging each other to make a bigger splash than the other.

The evenings we were alone were pleasant as well. We sat together under the stars, holding each other, swinging in our hammock. During the fall and winter we spent a lot of time at the cabin. Natalie and Jacob would join us quite often. Jacob loved the cabin, the mountain, and the woods. He liked being "in the sky." He especially loved the hollowed-out tree. It was his secret hideaway. Natalie spent most of her time with me, asking me to tell her my stories over and over. She never seemed to get enough of them, and she always had different questions to ask. Cobie loved to watch his grandchildren, and he would smile and laugh as they ran around playfully. Life became fuller with each passing day.

Late one rainy fall afternoon I received a phone call from Trey. My sister was ill, and she was asking for me. Cobie and I got onto the first flight we could catch and went to my sister's house. The entire time we were there I never left her side. I read to her like she did to me when we were kids, and I brushed her hair. She asked about my life, about my travels. She listened intently and didn't ask questions like Natalie did. She wanted to know about the cabin, and what had made it so special to me. She told me about her life as a prosecutor, and she told me about some of her cases. I had always thought being a lawyer was a dull job, but it wasn't. We looked through her wedding album. She was so beautiful and young then. When I looked at myself I saw a shroud of gloom. We looked through photos of her children growing up, and she had a story for each of them. The twins had been such a handful, and I had always considered them heathens, but she loved them every bit as much as I loved Reese. Trey had always been quieter, but he was independent and did as he wanted. He had never really left home though. I think he was afraid to leave his mother all alone. I hadn't felt this close to my sister in many, many years, not since we were children. We had grown up and gone in different directions.

She died early on a Sunday morning. When her husband died, she purchased two burial plots side by side so she could rest next to him for eternity, and that is where we buried her. The funeral was beautiful. She had

so many friends and colleagues. Trent
and Tansey were there. They had grown
up. Tansey came over and hugged me. I
looked at her and her twin brother
differently now after my sister's stories.
They weren't heathens, and they never
had been; just very rambunctious
children. After the funeral, everybody
came by my sister's house to pay their
respects. They were mostly lawyers and
judges, but some of her clients and other
people that I didn't know how they
knew her, came by. That evening Cobie
and I sat and talked with her children. I
could actually see her in Tansey. It was
pleasant spending this time with my
niece and nephews. I hadn't seen them
much after they were grown.

     Two days after the funeral was
the reading of the will. I wasn't sure
why my sister had wanted me there
except that I was her sister. My sister
was very meticulous and organized.
That is what made her a successful
lawyer. Her will was tedious and long.
She divided up her money evenly into
trusts for her children and left Trey the
house. She had even set up trust funds

for her future grandchildren. Finally, at the end of the reading, the lawyer handed me an envelope. I couldn't imagine what my sister had inside the envelope for me. I didn't open it then, but I took it back to her house with me. I went into her study and closed the doors. I sat down on the huge velvet chair she had in there, and I slowly opened the letter. Inside was an oval locket with a letter. The letter said…

To my dear sister,

I want you to know how much I love and admire you. You always followed your heart and your dreams. You did everything I wanted to, but was scared. You have always had such passion and courage. You have never been afraid to take off on a whim and follow your heart. I have always been sensible and organized, fastidious in everything I've accomplished. I could have never lived my life like you. I always had to know where I was going. I always had to have a plan. I admire your life and your family, and have lived vicariously through you. I have no regrets about my life and family. I loved my husband and children. I have had a great life and have accomplished much. Sometimes I just wish I could have been more like you. I see a lot of you in Trey. I worry about Trey now. He's growing older and needs stability and people who can understand him. On his own I'm afraid he would be lost. As a last request, I would like Trey to go home with you and live in Mom and Dad's house. He has always admired Reese, and would love to work for him.

I had the locket made many years ago, and have worn it daily. Please open it up and take a look inside. I give you this locket and all its memories.

With love,
Your sister, Emily

As I read the letter, tears rolled down my cheeks. I opened the locket. Inside was a picture of Emily and me as very small children. We are sitting in front of a huge Christmas tree opening each other's gifts. We were very small and pudgy. Emily's hair was long in chestnut locks and mine shorter with golden waves. We were both wearing lacy red Christmas dresses and black patent leather shoes. I held the locket to my chest and cried.

As my sister requested, Trey came home with us. He didn't complain, but was very excited about the prospect of working with Reese. Reese welcomed Trey, and he began to show him the business. Trey turned out to be quite competent in the area of finances. He had a way with numbers like I did, only he had more vision like Reese and Nikki. He also understood the law. I guess that is what happens when you are the child of two lawyers and have a lawyer for a sister. The three of them took the business to a new level. Reese had already expanded the business into the neighboring communities but now they bought a small chain of parts stores. Emily had left Trey quite an inheritance. He just needed guidance on what to do with it. Nikki and Reese offered that guidance. They took the small chain that was going out of business, and they completely turned it around.

Reese, Nikki, and Trey made so much money that Nikki finally got her beach house. The house was beautiful. It was located on a jagged cliff overlooking the Pacific Ocean. The side of the house facing the ocean was all glass and windows. Looking out of the windows all I could see was ocean. I couldn't see the beach down below the cliff. It looked and felt as though I was floating on the ocean. She loved to leave the windows open and listen to the sounds of the beach; the surf pounding the shore, the birds, and the constant sea breeze. The house was beautiful and the views were breathtaking. It had become their escape, their little piece of the world. It was kind of like the cabin had always been for Cobie and me.

I enjoyed having Trey around. He made our lazy evenings even more enjoyable. Natalie and Jacob liked him as well. He was like a big kid and would play and tease them. He would grab their knees and tickle them. This made them laugh hysterically. My sister was right; he was more like me than her. He wasn't afraid of doing things wrong. He took calculated chances, and he was successful. Every year on Emily and her husband's anniversary, Trey and I went to visit their graves. We laid down flowers and told them about our lives. I wanted my sister to know just how successful Trey was, and how important to my family he had become.

My grandchildren seemed to grow up so quickly. Natalie grew into a beautiful young woman. She was always spontaneous and dramatic, so Nikki had her take dance lessons, voice lessons, and then lessons on various instruments. Natalie was a natural. She decided she wanted to be a performing artist. She wanted to dance and sing on Broadway. She had always performed in school plays, talent shows, and even the community theater. On stage she was radiant and shined as brilliantly as the North Star. She could dance, sing, and play almost any musical instrument. She was perfect for her career choice, and I supported her. I told her to always follow her heart and not be afraid. At one time I had also dreamed of being an actress but, with the loss of Nathan, I had pulled myself away from acting. She also loved my car, and I allowed her to drive me around in it from time to time. She wanted glamour and fame, and my car represented that to her.

Jacob had grown into a very handsome young man. The girls adored him. He was quite a lady's man from an early age. Having an older sister, he was used to the attention he received from her and her friends. They always thought he was adorable, and they mooned all over him. When he was twelve, one of Natalie's friends, a cute blond girl with bright blue eyes, fair skin, and rosy cheeks, had the biggest crush on him. He had a crush on her as well. He wasn't shy around girls at all, and when they flirted with him he flirted back. Anyway, Nikki found him and the girl kissing in the backyard one Saturday afternoon. As Reese tells it, Nikki went white as a sheet, her eyes rolled up into her head, and she almost fainted. He had to catch her to keep her from hitting the ground. He thought it was hilarious, but Nikki kept a very close eye on Jacob after that. I don't think she let him out of her sight for more than thirty seconds at a time. He was a very good-looking boy and charming, and the girls couldn't keep their hands off him. They chased him everywhere. I knew one day, when he found the right girl, she wouldn't be chasing him. He would be chasing her.

Eventually Trey settled down and married an intense young lady who could be a shrewd businesswoman. She had jet-black hair and blue eyes. The color of her hair made her eyes appear to be a surreal shade of blue, like the color of the sky that day after the storm, tornado sky blue. She was very small and petite and not a soul would have guessed that she could have such a cunning mind. Together they were a good team and the business grew. They had no plans for children. They just wanted to make money; although they lived quite modestly, and they didn't seem to spend it frivolously on items of only material value. They had bought a three-bedroom condominium and decorated it lightly. Most of their time together wasn't spent at home but traveling on business or with Cobie and me. Her parents were both dead and she didn't have any family left, so she adopted us, Trey's family. We appreciated having her around and she became one of our family.

The elderly lady slept silently in her chair. Her chest slowly heaving in and out and the twinkle around her neck clearly a golden locket. The sun made its way to the peak of the mountain and began to shine, making way to dawn's earliest morning.

Memories

The next several years of my life were a twisting, turbulent journey loaded with memories. It was like a tumultuous crossing into the obscurities my life had held. Memories of life and loves departed. I found the answers to questions I didn't want to know, questions that I had long given up on finding any answers to, yet had never really looked. The answers had always been in front of my face, staring at me from beyond the grave, begging me to look further and find them.

Over the winter, Cobie had fallen ill. I first noticed that he had less energy to do our normal daily routines. He tired very easily. Then I noticed his breathing had become more labored, and he had developed a cough. My first reaction was that he had caught a nasty cold. I made him rest, stay inside, and I took care of him, but he didn't get any better. He progressively got worse. He was stubborn and refused to go to the doctor. Finally, Reese forced Cobie against his will to go to the emergency room. The doctors diagnosed him with pneumonia and kept him in the hospital. They gave him a room, and I stayed by his side. Reese, Nikki, and our grandchildren came by quite often to visit, but mostly it was me and Cobie. I wouldn't leave the hospital. I couldn't leave Cobie's side. He had been my entire life for many decades, and I refused to let him go now. I didn't even want to imagine my life without him.

His illness was touch and go for a while, and the doctors weren't sure if he was going to pull through. I was angry at him for not going to the doctor earlier, instead waiting until he felt so horrible and was so weak that his son had to take him. I was scared that he wasn't going to make it, and I didn't know how I could go on without him. I didn't think I could. I knew if he died so would I. My life would end with his. I wasn't ready to let that happen. We still had life to live. He couldn't leave me. I just wouldn't allow it.

After a couple of weeks, he started to get better, and he showed signs of progress. Finally he was able to leave the hospital and came home. At home he had to take it easy, and I continued to stay by him and care for him. Natalie would stop by every day after school and help us out. Sometimes she would cook or clean the house for us. Other times we would all sit together and play a card game or board games. She would also just sit and talk with Cobie. I didn't know what they talked about, but I didn't interfere. I liked to see the two of them spending time together. Cobie's illness made me realize we were getting very old, and we wouldn't have many more of these times together. I didn't want to obstruct any of the precious moments any of us had to share together.

It turned into spring, and Jacob would come over and mow the lawn and take care of our plants. He also spent time relaxing and visiting with us. He seemed to soak up every moment we had with him like a sponge. Reese had become very authoritative, as he feared for his father's health. He would stop by frequently to check on our health. I think Cobie's illness had made him realize how weak we were, and how susceptible to illness we had become in our old age. As his parents we had always been strong, and now he realized we weren't invincible; one day we wouldn't be around anymore. He wasn't about to let either of us go, and so he felt he had to control the situation. He took Cobie to every doctor's appointment, and he forced me as well to start going to the doctor regularly. He wanted to make sure we lived our lives to their fullest and didn't go prematurely.

Cobie made a full recovery physically, but mentally he was changed. He had been close to death, and for the first time he understood that he was not indestructible. We had never planned for our futures, but had gone in whatever direction life took us, and we had a wonderful life. There is no part of our life I would change, and I don't believe our lives could have or would have been better if we had planned everything out. I believed our life together was perfect. Cobie though had a new obsession with planning our future. There were a lot of loose ends that he didn't want to leave this earth left untied. When he or I left this earth he wanted everything tidy and organized for Reese, Nikki, and our grandchildren.

Technically we still owned the shop. Reese and Nikki ran it and had expanded on the business, but we still owned it, and the final decision was always ours. Reese and Trey had set up shares for us from their business venture, and we collected dividends. We still owned our parents' homes. We had our own home and the cabin. We had money in bank accounts and stocks that we knew we would never spend in the rest of our lifetime. We went to see a lawyer and had wills drawn up. It was a complicated process, but we decided to leave the business to Reese and Nikki. Our shares in the auto parts chain we had divided equally among Trey, his wife, Reese, and Nikki. We left my parents' home to Trey. The house had been left to Emily and me. When she died, it became mine. I felt he deserved to have it. It was a piece of his mother's life. Cobie's parents' house we left to Nikki, and our house we left to Jacob. Our money was divided up equally and left in trusts for our grandchildren. We wanted them to be able to follow their dreams without money getting in the way. Reese and Nikki were well off, and they had always taken very good care of their children but we wanted to leave them their own financial security. Any stocks that we had we divided and left equal amounts to Reese, Nikki, Trey, and his wife. The smaller items we hadn't made any decisions about yet. We also made arrangements for our deaths as well. We decided that in the event of our deaths we wanted to be cremated. We set aside a fund to pay for our cremations in the event of one or both of our deaths.

Our lives had become confined to our home and children. We no longer traveled together, not even to the cabin. Any trips we made to the cabin were accompanied by our family. We enjoyed our family trips wherever we went, but we didn't get much privacy. Reese wouldn't let us out of his sight. I felt like a child again; any moments Cobie and I had together felt like stolen moments. It was like we were children again, trying to sneak out of our parents' house through a bedroom window in order to not get caught.

Reese and Nikki never left town on business together. Usually Reese would go alone and have Nikki look after us. When they went on vacation, we went with them. We spent a lot of time at the beach house. I loved the beach house, and I would sit near the window wall with the windows open, watching the ocean, and listening to the sounds. I treasured the sounds of the birds and the surf beating against the shore. I enjoyed every minute of my life, even with the loss of my independence.

We had given in to Reese and allowed him to take care of us. I understood what was going through his mind. I remembered when my parents and Cobie's parents had gotten too old to take care of themselves, and how

Cobie and I had been there. We were always there for them. We didn't want them departing this world without knowing how much we loved and respected them. We didn't want them leaving alone, but we wanted to be there to hold their hands, and that is what we did. Now it was Reese's turn to show us just how much we meant to him.

Nikki loved helping out. She had been disappointed in her parents' decision on how to spend their remaining years. They had sold their house and moved into an assisted-living home. Clay had been in and out of the hospital with various medical difficulties, and Sammy had suffered a minor stroke. Nikki wasn't very happy with their decision. She wanted them to live with her and Reese. Sammy and Clay wouldn't have that though. They didn't want to be taken care of; they insisted on keeping their independence. From time to time we visited them, and they came over to visit with us. Neither of them could get around well anymore, and they didn't drive. Nikki and Reese would usually pick them up, and we would all get together and enjoy what moments we had left. The time we spent all together brings me some of my fondest memories. Sammy had been my best friend since elementary school, and I thought of her and loved her more as a sister. I truly couldn't have asked for more than I had been given in life. I had a wonderful husband who loved me more than anything else in life. We had raised a remarkable son who married my best friend's daughter. Together they had raised two amazing children. I had everything and really couldn't have asked for more.

Natalie had grown into an astonishing and remarkable young woman. She was accepted by a performing arts school in New York, and she was excited. She followed her dreams. She left for school the fall after she graduated high school. Life felt lonely without her. She had spent so much time with us. She would come by almost every day after school, and now we didn't see her much. I looked forward to her letters, and Cobie and I would read them together. It was one of the highlights in our lives. After Cobie's illness, Natalie and Cobie had formed a special bond. They talked quite seriously, like they were plotting the future of the world. I wondered what they could be talking about, but I didn't understand. When I tried to listen in, I couldn't make sense of what they were saying. They had a top-secret code between them. All I was ever able to make out was Houston, Texas, and something about a bank. I didn't get in the way. Cobie had changed since his illness, and I knew whatever he and Natalie were planning somehow had something to do with me. One day, when they were ready to tell, me I would find out. Until then, I allowed them to have their moments without my obstruction.

At school in New York, Natalie was in heaven. She met a young man with whom she attended school. His name was Tye. He was a songwriter and musician. She sent us pictures of the two of them. He had long blond hair and brown eyes. His eyes looked familiar. I had to stare at the pictures for a while to figure it out exactly, but his eyes reminded me of Nathan's. They were the same color and shape, and they had the same seriousness about them. Occasionally she would send us a song he wrote for her. We finally met him one summer after they had been dating for about a year and a half. He was vibrant like Natalie but he also had a solemn, dark side to him. His dark side wasn't physically evident, but I could feel it. I also felt it when I read the songs he wrote that Natalie had sent us. The resemblance he bore to Nathan was uncanny. He definitely had the same eyes. When I looked into them, I felt as though I was looking at Nathan. He was a mystery that I had to unravel.

I asked him about his family, and I learned that he had spent most of his childhood in North Carolina, and then he had moved to Maryland when he was a teenager. His mother had been a nurse, and his father an electrician. He was more than willing to share stories about his family with us. None of the stories he shared gave me any reason to believe he was Nathan's. They say that everybody has a twin. Maybe he was Nathan's, and there was nothing more to it. He was in a band, and they performed at various clubs in New York. He wrote most of the lyrics and music. They weren't famous yet, but he made enough to pay his way through school. He and Natalie appeared to be very much in love. She had never really had time for a boyfriend before, or she just wasn't interested, and had never been in a relationship with any boy that lasted more than a few dates. I knew there was something special about him to have grabbed her attention. I accepted and liked him. He was very polite and respectful. There was something mysterious and dark about him, and I seemed to be the only one who could feel it, I thought. I had a chat alone with Natalie before they left. She felt his dark side as well, and that is what had attracted her to him. He was a mystery to her, and she wanted to know the answers. She wanted to know everything about him.

Jacob grew into a very attractive and extremely charismatic young man.

He had no goals for his life and a black book thicker than the bible. He had more friends than I could keep up with and a different girlfriend every time we saw him. Nikki wasn't too happy about his flamboyancy with girls. She thought he was too young to be such a player. Reese just laughed and told her not to worry. He said one day Jacob would fall hard for the right girl, and then his life would be turned upside down. That didn't seem to make Nikki feel any better. Trey noticed his talent for charming people, and he gave Jacob a part-time job at one of the auto parts stores. Jacob liked his job, and he was good at it.

Being the son of a mechanic/body man and the grandson of a mechanic, he knew everything there was to know about cars. He didn't need to look up parts to tell customers what they needed, and he gave tips on how to complete difficult jobs. Jacob himself had never worked on a car but he had been born into it, and he had watched his father, grandfather, and other mechanics so much that he had seen them perform car miracles. The customers loved him, and they specifically asked for him. After Jacob graduated high school, Trey brought him into the business more, started teaching him the behind-the-scenes work, and taking him on sales trips. Jacob was a natural in sales because of his charm. He could sell anything to anyone including the most stubborn, pigheaded client. Jacob had found his niche in life. He enjoyed working for Trey and Trey, in turn, loved having Jacob around. Trey put him in the marketing and sales division where Jacob flourished.

The day started out as a normal perfect spring day. We slept in, had a late breakfast, then Reese called. He always called about the same time every day. He asked how we were doing, and then he reminded us he would be coming by late in the afternoon to pick us up. We were going to visit and have dinner with Sammy and Clay. We did this a lot on Wednesdays. After his call we went out and did some gardening—trimming the old blooms off our roses and trimming our out-of-control wisteria. The wisteria just grew and grew, and it bloomed almost all year. Every time we trimmed it, it grew more and bloomed again. The sky was clear, there was a light breeze, and the sun was bright. The birds were out everywhere, chirping and talking to one another, trying to find a mate. After we finished our gardening, we went back inside and got cleaned up. Reese came by about four. Nikki was already at her parents' home. She didn't work much anymore, but she spent most of her time checking on and taking care of her parents.

When we arrived at their apartment, an ambulance was there. I had seen other ambulances at other times that we had visited, but this time was different. Calmness had overcome me and it felt like a dream. I knew the ambulance was here for my friend. In slow motion I watched as they wheeled out Sammy on a stretcher with Nikki by her side. The paramedics loaded her into the back of the ambulance and Nikki and the paramedics helped her father into the ambulance as well. Then she ran over to Reese. She started crying hysterically. He calmly opened the car door for her, and we all got back into his car to follow the ambulance to the hospital. Everything was still playing in slow motion and I knew my friend was in a better place. Nikki thought she had another stroke, but nothing was confirmed yet. Nikki calmed down some, and she just continued to whimper as she tried to speak. When we got to the hospital Sammy was already gone. I knew in my heart that she was. Nikki ran over to her mother and father and cried on his shoulder while holding on to her mother's hand. Clay and Nikki sat there for what seemed like a very long time, holding and comforting each other.

Suddenly life sped up again and we were in a busy hospital with nurses rushing everywhere. I went over to Sammy but I didn't cry. I knew she was someplace better than this. If this had been another stroke, she would have never recovered. She would have completely lost her independence and probably suffered brain damage. I think she let herself go. Sammy would have never wanted to live in the condition this stroke would have left her in. I felt happy for her. We had a beautiful funeral for her and I visited her grave quite frequently. I placed flowers by her tombstone as I would reminisce with her about our lives from the times we were silly kids to what our grandchildren were up to now. Nikki put her foot down and insisted on her father coming to live with them. She quit working and hired a part-time nurse. Clay didn't argue or put up a fight. He knew his days were limited and wanted to spend them with his only child and grandson. He was heartbroken when his wife died, and a piece of him died with her, but he knew his time wasn't up yet, so he lived out the rest of his days to the fullest. Clay died of natural causes about a year later. I believe he was finally ready to join his wife, Sammy.

Life went on quite typically, although I felt a void without my best friend. Even though we didn't see them as much since they had moved into an assisted-living home, we still talked three to four times a week. Natalie came home a couple of times a year to visit, and she came home for her grandparents' funerals. Tye had come with her for the funerals. He admired her close relationship with her grandparents. His father had been orphaned and he only had his mother's parents. He said that he didn't ever know them very well. His grandfather had died before he was born and his grandmother lived in a home. His parents weren't close to them. He had seen his grandmother only a couple of times. I thought this odd, and I asked Natalie about his grandparents. She didn't know much, as Tye never really talked about them. All she knew was there had been a tragic event that had torn his family apart. His mother had left home at a young age to get away from it. She didn't want to pry into his painful past, and she hoped that one day he would feel comfortable enough to talk about it.

Jacob was a busy young man. He had the sales department under control, and he was making a lot of money for the company. He wasn't such a player anymore. He had channeled his charm and energy into the business. He had everyone wrapped around his finger. He came by to visit every couple of weeks, and he told us about his new ideas and enterprises. Trey and his wife were doing well. They were ecstatic about the changes Jacob had brought the company. They felt freed of some of the business, and they decided it was time to have a baby.

Late one night, Cobie had already gone to bed and I was on my way when there was a knock on the door. It was Nikki. When I opened the door I noticed tears in her eyes. She wrapped her arms around me and hugged me. I had become her surrogate mom since Sammy had died. I had always been a second mom to her, but I never took Sammy's place in her heart; lately she came to me more and more. This night she just needed someone to be with who knew her mother as well as she did or maybe even better. We sat down on the couch and talked about her parents. She missed them a great deal. I took out some photo albums that I had taken from my parents' house after their deaths. In the albums were pictures of Sammy, Sarah, and me as kids. In the photos we were playing dress up and having slumber parties and birthdays. Nikki loved looking at the pictures of her mom and she began to smile. Some of them were photos of me in plays and there was the photo taken at the prom.

It was the only prom I had gone to and Sammy hadn't been there. I had only been there because I was Nathan's date and he was two years ahead of me in school. When she saw the photo she suddenly developed a strange look and twisted her face up. Then she asked me about him. I had never talked about Nathan to anybody, even after finding his Purple Heart. We had simply placed it on the mantel to pay him respect. I told her the story about how we had dated, and how he had gone to war and never come home. I even took his

Purple Heart off the mantel and showed it to her.

She said, "Tye looks like this boy only with blond hair." I had noticed that as well. She asked if he had any relatives. I told her how he had an older brother and a twin sister. I had never met his brother, and I hadn't really been friends with his sister. They were close but as teenagers had separate lives. She seemed intrigued by this mystery. Something had suddenly taken hold of her, and the old focused Nikki was back. She went home, and I went to bed.

As I lay down beside Cobie, I noticed his breathing seemed very shallow and his heartbeat irregular. I had spent many, many years listening to his breathing and heartbeat, falling asleep to it, and something was wrong. I didn't sleep much that night, but I spent most of it counting the seconds between each heartbeat and each breath he took. I wrapped myself around him.

The following morning I took him to the doctor. He had in infection in his lungs. He was admitted to the hospital, but there wasn't much they could do. At his age his body wasn't strong enough to fight the infection, and he didn't want to spend the remainder of his life hooked up to machines in a hospital. So we took him home. I called Natalie. Once she finished her final exams she flew home. She missed her own graduation to be with her grandfather for his final days. For the next few days everybody was at my house, doting on Cobie and me. They were both the happiest and saddest days of my life. I had the strength of my family, but I was about to lose my life. I was ready for him to go, but I wanted to go with him. I lay by his side and told him how much I loved him. He gave me a small box, and he asked me not to open it until he died. I put the box aside, and I told him when he died I would be with him. He wasn't going alone. He urged me to not give up yet. There was something inside the box I needed before I could join him. He said it was the *key to the answer I needed before I could pass.*

I didn't know what he meant, but if I had anything to do with it, he wasn't going without me. As I lay by his side, his breathing stopped. My heart shattered into a million jagged pieces of glass that coursed through every vein in my body. I closed my eyes and welcomed my own death. I envisioned Cobie's spirit rising above me with his silly smile. He was now a young man once again, and he was handing me the box. The next thing I knew I heard Natalie saying, "Gram, everything will work out, it's going to be all right." I wasn't in heaven with Cobie. I was still here on earth lying in my bed beside my husband. I took her hand and she held me. She said it wasn't my time yet; we had something to do first.

As Cobie had wished, he was cremated and we had a service for him. With Cobie's ashes I had a small urn made for Reese, and I had my own urn, containing his ashes, that I kept close to me at all times. After the service, Reese and Nikki urged me to go home with them, but I refused. I needed to be in my home with Cobie. Really, I wanted to be up in the cabin where I knew I could feel Cobie's strong presence, but I settled for my own home. Reese and Nikki then decided to go home with me.

That night, after everybody was in bed, Natalie came into my room. I hadn't been able to sleep, and I welcomed her. She handed me the box and told me to open it. I hadn't forgotten about the little box. I simply didn't want to open it. Whatever was inside could only be meaningless without Cobie. I took the little box and held in it my hands. I then tried to hand it back, asking her to open it. She said that she couldn't; only I could open it. What was inside was only meant for me. I stared at the box for a while. I knew whatever was in this box was what Cobie and Natalie had been planning. I had to open it—*it was the key to the answers I needed*—before I could join Cobie. All I wanted was to be with Cobie. So I opened the box. Inside was a key to a safety deposit box. He couldn't make anything simple and small for me even in his death. His surprises and gifts for me had always been theatrical. He knew me and had something waiting for me in this box that I needed. I couldn't imagine what but I took the key. It was attached to a chain. Natalie said I had to pack my bags; we would be leaving in the morning. I didn't know how, since Reese and Nikki watched me like two hawks, but we packed a bag for me and she took it out and placed it in the trunk of my car.

The next morning as I awoke I heard Natalie talking with her parents. As I became more alert I noticed they were arguing not talking. Nikki was saying, "There is no way you and your grandmother can be taking this trip. What about your life in New York and what about your grandma's health?" Unfortunately, I was in perfect health, which was why my body refused to die with Cobie's.

Reese finally spoke up and said, "They have to take the trip. Dad planned it that way." Nikki relented but gave Natalie strict orders to call them daily, once in the morning and once every evening. She agreed. I couldn't believe my family was arguing about me. I was a grown woman and had been for many years. I knew as well as Reese and Natalie that we had to make this trip and fulfill Cobie's wishes. I would never be able to move on unless we did. So I got up, had breakfast, took a shower, and placed my key around my neck. I also placed three items in my largest purse that had significant value to me at this juncture in my life. First was Cobie's urn. I wasn't going anywhere without him. Second was the cell phone that Reese had given me after Cobie's first illness, and last was Nathan's Purple Heart.

Nikki gave me a long hug and told me, "I love you very much; you are the only mother I have left and I couldn't stand for anything to happen to you." Reese held me. He didn't say anything, he just held me. I knew he loved me, and we both knew that I wasn't coming back. This was it. Then we left. We stopped to see Jacob. I couldn't leave without giving my playboy a hug and telling him how much I loved him. Then we made a small stop to visit Trey and his wife before we drove to the bank.

They took us into a room full of safety deposit boxes and took out the one that belonged to me. I took the key off my neck, carefully unlocked the box, and opened it. Inside, the first thing that caught my eyes was a picture of me sitting on the beach alone as a young woman. There was also a long note in Cobie's writing. The note said…

To my dearest wife,

I have always loved you with all my heart and soul. The years I spent away from you were the worst in my life. There are things I learned in my years apart from you that I knew you didn't want to know. Now you need to know. You need to know everything. I had assumed you married Nathan, and only found out you hadn't when one of my coworkers told me he was believed to be taken a prisoner of war. His helicopter had been shot down by enemy fire, and his body hadn't been recovered. When I learned this, I went back home to find you, but you weren't there. Your parents told me you were traveling the country, and showed me their latest postcard from you. I started there and went to find you, but you had already moved on, so I traced your footsteps for six months. I didn't believe I would ever

*find you, and was ready to turn back when I
spotted you on a beach. I was sitting under a
canopy having a drink when you caught my
eye. I didn't know what to say to you. How
was I supposed to tell you that Nathan was
gone and I was here? For hours I sat there
having one drink after the next, trying to get
up the nerve to talk to you. I had chased you
for months and now I had found you, but I
couldn't speak to you. Instead, I just sat at
the bar getting drunker and drunker. You
were so beautiful. The wind would catch
your golden waves and send them flying.
You'd tickle your toes in the water and wait
for the waves to wash over your body. I
watched you until long after the sun set.
You stayed on the beach until the cool
night's breeze came in, and then you left. I
didn't follow you, but left as well. I went to
the mountains. I hiked to the top, and stayed
there so long I lost track of time. The
mountain had helped me clear my head and
think straight. I had been stupid, and felt I
wasted my last chance to ever see you. That
spot on the mountain where I camped is the
spot I later had the cabin built on. I knew I
had to find you again, so I went to Las
Vegas to gamble any money I had left on the*

chance I would make more and could renew my search for you.

I saw you come into the casino, and I couldn't believe it was you. I knew then that I had a second chance. Unfortunately, you were drunk. I followed you from casino to casino and walked closely behind you. I had to make sure nothing happened to you, but I didn't want to speak to you drunk. I wanted to speak to you sober. Eventually you stumbled into a casino and sat down. I thought you were going to pass out, but you didn't. You focused yourself on something, and I watched. You had focused yourself on another gambler, a man at the slots. When he left, you went over to the slot machine he had been at and won the jackpot. You put the ticket in your pocket and walked my way. You came right up to me, and kissed me like nothing had ever happened. Like I hadn't been searching for you for months and racking my brain about how to tell you what I knew. You just came up, kissed me, and asked me how to play roulette. We went to the table and played, and you kept winning until you passed out on a couch. I checked out two connecting rooms, and put you to bed. Then I went back, gambled, and *thought about everything. I was so confused. I knew I had to see you in the morning.*

The next morning I waited for you to get up, but you had been so plastered the night before you wouldn't get up. I waited, and then knocked on your door. You didn't make a sound. I didn't want to come into your room and scare you. I knew you wouldn't remember the night before, so I went downstairs and ate. That is when I saw you sneaking out of the hotel and running down the street. I couldn't help but laugh at your behavior. Eventually you stopped at a diner, went in, and sat down. After a few minutes I followed you in, but you weren't at your table, so I sat down and waited for you. Now that you were sober I wasn't sure what to expect, but you seemed happy to see me.

When we left I had planned on telling you everything, but you wouldn't let me. You were so hardheaded you wouldn't even let me show you the money you had won. How could I tell you? Then I thought that maybe you already knew, maybe that is why you ventured across the country alone. I knew I couldn't let my second chance go. So I never brought up what I knew until you found the Purple Heart. I don't know any more about Nathan than I've told you but I found his sister. She lives in a nursing home in Texas. I want you and Natalie to go to her, talk to her. You need to know exactly what happened to Nathan. Then you need to retrace your footsteps on the journey you took me that led me across the country to you. I want you to tickle your toes in the water and take a look behind you. That is where I sat and watched you. When you have completed the trip I am asking you to follow, go to the cabin, and pour my ashes over the mountain. I want them to follow the wind. I will be with you wherever you go,

Love,
Cobie

I cried as I started to read the letter but as I read on I couldn't help but laugh. I had been very hardheaded, and he was right; I wouldn't have listened to him. I wasn't ready to know about Nathan. Natalie knew exactly where Nathan's sister was, and we left for Texas.

The journey to Texas only lasted a few days, but I wasn't sure what to say to this woman I hadn't seen in decades and never really knew. Would she recognize me? Would she hate me? When we arrived, a nurse escorted us to her. She had headphones on her ears and was listening quietly to something on a CD. We sat down, and she turned off the CD. I introduced myself. She smiled at me and asked what had taken me so long. I hadn't been sure what to expect, but now I was glad I was here.

Cobie was right; I needed to know the answers. She said Nathan had loved me very much and spoke of me in every letter. She was sometimes jealous that he seemed to miss me more than her, his twin sister. Shortly after I left for college they received word that Nathan's helicopter had been shot down, and his body hadn't been recovered. Their mother took it the hardest. She couldn't accept that her boy was lost in a foreign country, maybe even a prisoner. Slowly she went insane. Their father decided they should move, hoping to help his wife get a grip on life. So they moved to Texas. Nathan's sister did not move with them, as she couldn't stand to see what had happened to her family. It hurt her to be with them.

The move seemed to help her mother at first, but she never really recovered. She spent hours and even sometimes days crying. A couple of years after her parents moved to Texas, her mother died. She took an overdose of prescription medication. Nathan's sister then moved to Texas. Not long after she moved, a man came by their home. He introduced himself as Turtle, a friend of Nathan's. I had remembered reading about Turtle in Nathan's letters. He gave Nathan's father Nathan's dog tags. Her father then became enraged and yelled at the young man until he left.

She went after him, wanting to know more. She wanted to know why he had her brother's dog tags. She caught up to him and they walked and talked. He didn't know why he had the dog tags. He couldn't remember. He had suffered brain damage and permanent amnesia after the explosion. He had been on the helicopter as well, but he had somehow lived. He couldn't remember much. The next thing after the explosion that he remembered was wandering around enemy territory where he was picked up and placed in some type of camp. At first he thought it was a nightmare because he couldn't remember why he was even there in this place and not at home. His mind had blocked the war completely. He slowly began to remember some things, but not everything, and he didn't know exactly how much time he had spent at this enemy camp. Eventually they loosened up security at the camp, and then they left all together. He and the others made their escape and found that the war was over. He made his way out of the country and back to America.

He hadn't any family, as his parents had died when he was very young. He had been orphaned and spent most of his childhood in homes. That is why he joined the military as soon as he could. He didn't know where else to go but here to return the dog tags. She checked out his story and found that Nathan had been "buried." They had his body exhumed. The body turned out to be that of Nathan. He had died that day in the helicopter explosion. He had never left me, and I had never left him. The war had taken us away from each other. It destroyed him, his mother, and his entire family. Nathan's father wanted nothing to do with this young man. He blamed his wife's insanity and suicide on him. That is when Nathan's father mailed me his Purple Heart and wrote me a letter. I had never checked the package for a letter.

Nathan's sister though felt very differently about the young man, and they got to know each other better, eventually marrying and raising three children. Her father couldn't accept their marriage and refused to speak with her. She told us about her children, two boys and a girl. Her sons still lived in Texas, and they came to visit every so often, but her daughter had left as soon as she turned eighteen. She had moved to North Carolina, put herself through school, and became a registered nurse. She got married and had a child. She didn't visit very often. She didn't understand how two people who should love each other didn't speak. She was upset at her parents and her grandfather. He was her only grandfather, and she never knew him. She had tried to see him, but he turned her away. He had become a very bitter man after losing Nathan and his wife, and then he felt… his daughter.

Her daughter came home for her grandfather's funeral. She wasn't married yet, had come alone, and then turned around and went back to North Carolina immediately following the funeral; she didn't stay and visit. She visited every few years because of her son. She didn't want him to not know his grandparents. Although Nathan's sister's husband had died soon after their grandson's birth.

Natalie and I looked at each other, and I asked if she had any pictures. She brought us to her room and first showed us a picture of the young man, Turtle, who she married. I recognized his face immediately. He had been the man in the park. He was the reason I wandered the country and found Cobie. He was it! I had never expected to see his face

again, but it was etched in my brain.
Did he know me? As much as Nathan
spoke of me did he know who I was? I
asked her if he had remembered Nathan
ever speaking of me. He not only had
remembered Nathan speaking of me but
he had a picture of me that she had
kept. It was tattered and war torn, but it
was me. He said Nathan had kept it
close to his heart. He didn't know how
he had ended up with it any more than
he knew why he had Nathan's dog tags.
He had to have recognized me that day.
Why hadn't he said anything to me,
even after I spilled my guts to him about
Nathan? Maybe he just couldn't tell me
what had happened, or he didn't think
it was important to dwell on the past,
but was more important to move
forward. After she showed us the
pictures of Turtle and me she took out
pictures of her children and
grandchildren. Just as Natalie and I
suspected, Tye was her grandchild.

We had visited for a few hours and
left when visiting hours were over, but
Natalie told her she would be back and
very soon. She immediately called Tye

and frantically asked him to get on the next plane to Houston, Texas. Within twenty-four hours he was with us in Texas. We picked him up at the airport, and she told him the entire story on our way to the nursing home. Natalie had taken the information and run with it. My mind was still trying to digest the bits and pieces. Nathan died and yet somehow from beyond the grave he had watched over me. Our lives had been entangled in some webbed path. A path I hadn't known I was following.

I felt as if I hadn't made the choices in my life but Nathan had designed my life from beyond his grave. He was my guardian angel who watched over me and made sure I made the right decisions. He had sent my Natalie to Tye. He couldn't have chosen a more wonderful young lady for his great nephew. Tye's entire family had been ripped apart because of what had happened to him, and somehow Natalie and I were the answer to putting everything right again. They say loved ones who die are always with you in spirit. Until now I had never fully understood that phrase. I had always felt the presence of my parents, Emily, and Sammy after they had left. They were a part of me, and they lived in my heart. I didn't know someone could adjust the flow of another person's life from the grave. Nathan had always been with me even when I wasn't with him, when I had thought he left me. That was my excuse for not being able to face a tragedy that my immature mind couldn't yet process. I had learned to deal with death much better after losing my parents and Cobie's parents. He had been with me. He sent Cobie messages, me messages, and now Natalie. I had always had two men: Nathan, who was strong and diligent, and Cobie, who was my one true love. I could feel them both in the car with me now, Nathan's firm grasp on one side and Cobie's heart beating with mine on the other. I could feel his breath on my neck. We finally arrived at the nursing home.

Inside we were greeted again by the staff and taken to her room. Visiting hours would be over shortly so we didn't have much time. When Tye entered the room she looked as though she had seen a ghost. Natalie and I left them alone to talk, and we waited just down the hall in the waiting room. When visiting hours were almost up we went back; the two of them were still talking. I had something to give Tye before we left. I still had Nathan's Purple Heart, and it didn't belong to me anymore. It belonged to him. I took it out of my purse and handed it to him. He looked at me much the way Nathan used to, and he opened the box. I told him it was now his to be treasured. His great uncle was a strong and courageous man, and he never would have wanted his family torn apart over him. Tye was trying to be strong, but I could tell he was ready to cry. He kissed his grandmother good-bye, and we left. When we got outside he held Natalie for a very long time, and I believe he cried, although he covered it well.

We stopped and had something to eat, and then we went back to our hotel for the night. The next day we took Tye to the airport, and he flew back to New

York. Natalie and I headed back to the nursing home for one last visit. When we got there they informed us that she had passed the previous night. We stayed for her funeral, and Tye again flew back to Houston to be there. His whole family showed up, and I was able to meet her other children and grandchildren. She had a beautiful family, and everybody seemed to be at peace. I had not only followed Cobie's wishes but I had followed those of Nathan. It was as if Nathan had told Cobie what needed to be done to bring his family back together — to right everything wrong that had happened. After we left Houston I had to visit Nathan's grave before we could follow the rest of Cobie's wishes. We flew to Washington, DC, and visited Arlington National Cemetery. I apologized for lacking faith in him, and I thanked him for helping to guide my life. I could feel Nathan's spirit with me, and then it was suddenly gone.

We left Washington, DC, and we followed my zigzag path across the country. I had no rhyme or reason to the places I went and visited in my youth. I would just decide one day that I wanted to go somewhere, and then I'd go. No wonder it had been so difficult for Cobie to find me. There had been no logic to my travels. Natalie was more amazed than ever with my journey. The stories had always fascinated her, and now here she was with me. I described everything for her as we traveled. I didn't leave out any details, city to city and state to state. I told her all the events that happened and why I would end up at each new place. We finally arrived on the beach. It was a winter day, but here on the beach in sunny Florida, who would guess? This was the beach Cobie had written about in his letter and we found the bar he sat in as he watched me.

Natalie took my hand and we went out on the beach to the ocean. We kicked off our shoes and let the water wash over our feet and ankles. Then we walked along the beach at the edge of the water. The tide rolled in and covered our feet, and then it went back out. Finally we walked back to my spot and

sat down in the sand. We sat with our
legs in front of us and our toes pointed
toward the water. We wiggled our toes
in the sand, and then we waited for the
tide to roll in over us. As the tide rolled
in higher and higher the sun began to
set. I looked behind us, and I could see
Cobie sitting with a drink in his hand
and a smile on his face. He had a perfect
view of me from where he sat.

When the sun had completely set,
we walked up the beach and into the
bar. We sat down at the table I had seen
Cobie at and we talked over a drink. I
noticed our server was a young woman
of ethnicity I couldn't place, possibly
Asian and Middle Eastern. She was
beautiful with long thick straight brown
hair and bright emerald-green eyes. She
had recognized us as grandmother and
granddaughter, and she thought it was
wonderful that we were vacationing
together. Her comment made me look at
Natalie as if I was looking at myself. She
was about the same age I had been
when I first visited this beach, and for a
minute I saw myself through Cobie's
eyes. After we finished our drink, we

walked back to the car and drove to the hotel. We stayed up, opened the sliding door to the balcony so we could hear the surf, and played cards all night.

Our next stop on our trip was Las Vegas. I showed Natalie the casino I had gambled in and as many other casinos I could remember that I stopped in. I showed her the diner where Cobie had found me. We stopped in and had dinner, and I told her the story the way I remembered it. Next, I showed her the little chapel where Cobie and I had gotten married. The place was still around. We went in and looked at their photos. The one of Cobie and me after twenty-five years was still in one of their photo albums. Then we checked into the hotel where Cobie and I had stayed, and we went downstairs to do some gambling. I was old, and I felt if I was here I might as well gamble and make the most of my life. Cobie also would have wanted that. I still had my magic touch and Natalie wasn't bad. She won a little money, mostly at the slots. After we gambled for a while and had one or two drinks we headed back to our room. I was tired. I offered her money to continue gambling but she declined. She said she would rather be with me.

We watched some TV. I pondered the last few months' events in my brain. I had always known just how much Cobie loved me, but I couldn't have fathomed that he followed me across the country from one end to the next trying to find me. I knew I fell asleep that night with a smile on my face. I thought of Cobie following my patternless trail across America. It was more than destiny. Our lives had been set on a crash course to collide with one another.

The next day we headed to the cabin. We spent almost the entire day in the car and arrived just as the sun set. It was a cold night and I could tell snow was in the air. We had stopped at a small store before going up to the cabin. We bought some food, and Natalie insisted on fresh flowers. Cobie had asked her to put fresh flowers in the vase on the table. The cabin was cold inside but Natalie made a fire. We warmed ourselves in front of it. Then she got up and made some dinner. We ate at the little table, and then we sat in the twin rockers and looked out at the mountain in front us. It was an amazing sight that even after all these years and trips the cabin had never bored me. Both of us were weary from our travels and ready to settle in for the night.

The next morning Natalie made us breakfast and coffee. After breakfast, I took out Cobie's urn and we scattered his ashes over the mountain. The cold wind picked up most of them, and we watched them blow away. They went wherever the wind took them. I imagined them blowing over the mountain and valley, across the country, and over the seas. They were free. I could tell it was only a matter of time before the snow began to fall, and I asked her to go back home to her parents. She had given me everything Cobie had asked and more. Now she needed to leave and get back home safely before the snow came. The snows on the mountain could be treacherous, especially in my car. She held me and said, "I love you, Gram." Then she followed my wishes and got into my car and headed back down the mountain. I watched her until I could no longer see my little car, and then I headed back into the cabin.

There was a lot to be done. First, I knew when I didn't call Reese he'd be calling me. I also knew that soon the roads would be too dangerous for travel. So I picked up my phone and left a message, "Reese, I sent Natalie home. I'm at the cabin. It's time for me to join your father. I love you very much." Then I turned off my phone and placed it on the dresser. There was a safe underneath the floorboards that nobody but Cobie, Jacob, and I knew about. I lifted up the floorboards and opened the safe. As I had suspected, Cobie left me a note. It simply said …

I love you and I know I'll see you soon,

Love, Cobie

I took the note and placed it on Cobie's chair. Then I placed my folded $100 bill wedding ring inside the box. I went outside and placed the key to the safe inside the hollowed-out tree, and then I went back into the cabin. I sat down at the table with a pen and paper, and I decided what to do with all our small items of value that we hadn't decided on before. I left the cabin to Jacob. That is why I had left the key in the tree. He loved the tree, and I knew he would find the key there. I wanted my charmer to have my very special ring. Next I left my car to Natalie. She loved my car, and it suited her. I had left my bag of goodies from my travels in the trunk. I left Cobie's truck to Reese, as he was the one who gave it TLC and turned it into a hot rod. I left my gold and diamond wedding ring to Nikki. She was like a daughter to me, and I wanted her to have this piece of me. Last, I left my locket that Emily had given me to Trey. I wanted him to have this piece of me and his mom. I left my last wishes on the table. I closed all the curtains except the one in front of the rockers, I stoked the fire, sat down in my chair, and began to rock as I watched the snow gently fall upon the earth.

Epilogue

*T*he sun was shining brightly and fully overhead. Fires from the chimneys that had begun to die out were now reborn. Their smoke piled out into the fresh morning air. Food could be smelled as people fried eggs and bacon, and coffee brewed inside their cabins. Children were starting to come out and play in the snow, having snowball fights, and building snowmen. There was also a truck slowly, carefully making its way up the mountain. The road had been completely covered from the snowfall the night before. The driver seemed to know exactly where he was even though the road couldn't be seen. It was like he had traveled the road many times in the past. As the truck crept up the twisting road, it passed many cabins. Two figures could be seen in the cab, a man and a woman. The man had golden hair and ocean-blue eyes, and the woman had dark brown hair. The truck kept on until it reached the top.

The man and woman got out and ran up to the little cabin. Smoke was no longer flowing from the chimney, and the elderly lady could be seen in her chair from the outside. The couple went in, and the young man ran over to the chair, laid his head down on the elderly lady, and wept. The woman knelt beside him and wept with him.

The End…

Prologue

St. Augustine, 1823

Cara shivered, the stone cold floor beneath her. Shrieks sliced through the air above her, echoing through the stone walls. A moldy stench, thick in the surrounding air, drifted up her nostrils. The temperature dropped several degrees as a breeze touched her head. She dared to open her eyes and stare into the darkness surrounding her, peeling one eye open and then the next.

"Cara," sounded a soft voice, almost a whisper. A warm touch caressed her hand, a shadowy figure flashed before her eyes. "You need to leave." The soothing voice didn't elicit fear but warmth and love. Her eyes searched for whom it belonged to. A breeze brushed against her and the voice whispered in her ear. "You need to go. I can lead you."

She tilted her head and gazed upon a transparent woman, no more than twenty. Her flaxen hair fell across her shoulders, circling her heart-shaped face. "Who are you?" Cara stammered.

"I'm Alda, once like you. They've been here for centuries, before the pirates, before the first settlement. The true first inhabitants of this continent."

"Who are they?"

"They are Bloodseekers. Come now!" The urgency in her voice resounded inside Cara. She jumped to her feet and followed the apparition. Alda's white bodice hugged her torso, the black hem grazing the stone floor.

Light from candles illuminated the darkness as they wound through a narrow passageway, as one candle lit ahead of them, the one behind went dark. The brightness of each light cast a glow on the shadow beside it, lighting the faces of each ghost. One apparition after another, men and women, blood drenching their shirts and bodices from the fang marks in their necks. The chilly air sent waves of shivers spiraling through Cara's body. She lifted her arm to touch a girl, no more than twelve, but her hand went through the child's face.

They came upon a fork in the passage, Alda motioned for her to stop. Quickening footsteps sounded from the right. "Plaster yourself against the wall, into the shadows. They see heat, our lack of it will protect you."

Cara did as asked. Not questioning Alda. She knew the footsteps belonged to a Bloodseeker. One had come into her home and killed her family, draining them of every drop of blood. She tried to escape, to run, but he was too quick. His dark eyes bored into hers. And a voice inside her head commanded her to stop. Her body froze in place. She tried to move but his mind controlled the core of her brain and she collapsed, waking up on the stone floor.

Her mind swarming back to the present, she pressed herself against the wall, the shadowy apparitions swarmed around her, blanketing her in darkness, shielding her from the Bloodseeker. His footsteps halted at the fork, as if deliberating which direction to go. He turned and followed the corridor leading to the room she'd left, he halted. His black eyes glowed through the shadows surrounding her. She closed her eyes tight, to avoid his mind commands and held her breath. Cara stayed as motionless as possible, controlling the tremors threatening to shake her body.

Her sense of hearing heightened with her eyes squeezed shut, she heard his footsteps walk away from her and continue through the corridor. She popped her eyes open and watched his form through the corner of her eye. When he disappeared around the corner, Alda motioned for her to follow. *He'd know she wasn't there. He'd look for her.* The apparitions parted as Cara moved away from the wall.

Alda floated up the stairwell as Cara followed with gentle footsteps, careful not to draw his attention. A wooden door appeared before Cara as she reached the top of the stairs. Alda motioned for her to open it, the hinges creaking as she pushed it.

Moonlight from the crescent moon streamed through the parted heavy curtains, bathing the room in enough light that Cara could see. Dozens of ghosts swarmed the room. Now, able to see them clearly, she gasped. Their skin tones and origins varied - black, white, and varying shades of brown. None older than her. Their styles of dress told her many lived centuries before her. A young black ghost hovered in front of her, clothed in a thick graying dress. Her gentle brown eyes sent a burst of warmth through Cara's quaking, goose-pimpled body.

Alda soared towards a bookshelf and pointed to a nondescript brown leather book. "Pull it."

Cara hurried towards the shelf and lifted the book, the shelf easing back to reveal another room.

"Take the book inside the room. The door will close behind you."

Cara didn't argue. Thundering sets of footsteps pounded the floor behind her, only moments from catching her she dived into the room. The book case closed, leaving behind all the ghosts except Alda. A Bloodseeker rushed towards it, catching it with his hand. He forced the heavy door open. Cara scooted away from his grasp.

A bright red light flickered from the corner of the dark room. "Grab the light!" Alda yelled. Cara scurried towards it, dropping the book as she reached for it. She held it firmly in her hand and tugged, but the object was caught on something she couldn't see in the dark.

The Bloodseeker dived for her, catching her other arm in his firm grasp. A blast of white light diffused through the room from the object Cara clutched in her hand. He pulled her towards him. She tightened her grasp as the object and the nail it was stuck on slackened from the wall. The Bloodseeker, too late to stop her, screamed in agony as the light blasted him against the door, his body engulfed in flames.

The light enveloped Cara, pushing its way through her body. She burst into fire, the flames licking the walls, then eddying into nothingness. Her ginger hair now crimson red, her amber eyes shining as garnets in the darkness. Beneath her skin, muscles exploded to the surface.

"What's happening?"

A smile widened on Alda's face. "You're the one. We've waited for you."

"What do you mean and how come I can see you and they can't?"

"You are a Slayer, that's why you see us. As long as you wear the amulet you will be indestructible and invisible to the Bloodseekers. They won't be able to harm you. Your job is to find others like yourself and slay every last Bloodseeker. Don't ever take it off and keep it protected beneath your clothes. Should it fall into their hands they will use it against you. You see us because you are special. All the answers are in the book. Take it, place the amulet around your neck and leave now!"

Cara leaned over and grabbed the book. She then pulled the glowing amulet over her head. "What about you and the others?"

"You have freed us. We are forever grateful but you must leave."

Cara hurried towards the door, stepping on the Bloodseeker's ashes. The door opened for her and she ran through the house, ghosts guiding her way. She dodged the Bloodseekers, their dark glowing eyes searching, fangs sharp as daggers protruding from their upper gums. Their blood covered mouths saturated the air with the scent of iron. Claw-like fingers sliced through the air, scratching her clothes as she sprinted past them, hurdling tables and furniture with skill and agility unknown to her.

Finally, reaching the front entrance, she twisted the golden knob on the large, chunky door and ran into the morning's first light. Dawn. The sun rising just above the horizon. She stepped onto the porch, Bloodseekers on her trail. Stumbling down the steps, she landed face first in the dirt. Scrambling she lifted herself upright and quickly turned towards the house.

A tall, thin Bloodseeker hissed, shielding his face as he sank into the house, flames licking his hands. The sun's light rose bigger and brighter in the sky, immersing the house in radiance. The ground shook. She sprinted.

Reaching the relative safety of the tree line, she turned in time to watch the ground part around the house, swallowing it. Thousands of lights glowed as the ghosts swirled into the atmosphere, rising high into the sky as they disappeared. Screams reverberated in the air surrounding her as the Bloodseekers were burned and buried.

She cupped her ears and knelt, curling her head towards her knees to muffle their death screeches. Unable to stifle the noise, tears rose to her eyes from the pain in her throbbing ears. As soon as the screeching began, it stopped, and the earth filled in above the house. The ground appeared undisturbed. The sun shone high in the sky, erasing the dreadful night.

Cara lifted the amulet hanging against her chest, a large red stone set in the center surrounded by, and hanging on, a silver chain. She clutched it, the book tucked beneath her arm, and marched down the road. Not a soul peered outside their windows or took notice of the event.

The house was wiped from existence and erased from St.

Augustine's inhabitants' minds. Cara's secret.

Chapter 1

Alison

Music surging from the apartment next door startled Alison awake. Her body rolled off the couch with a soft thump, landing on an assortment of throw pillows she'd kicked off during her nap. She pulled herself off the floor and rubbed the sleep from her eyes. Mouth dry as the Sahara, she headed towards the kitchen for water. A shrill female scream vibrated against her eardrums, causing her to jump and drop her empty tumbler. It crashed to the floor with a loud thunk, mimicked by the shattering glass outside her front door.

The apartment complex was always quiet, especially after dark. It had to be the new neighbors. After sunset, they'd moved into the adjoining apartment. As a lonely girl in a new city, she'd watched them with admiration. Two women, neither over the age of twenty-five, single women living on their own.

One with long, brown wavy hair and eyes bluer than any she'd seen before. A surreal blue. The other girl had blonde highlights throughout the light brown hair, framing her flawless face and intense green eyes. Both had curves in the right places.

Self-conscious, she had compared her still developing body to their mature ones. Her gut swelled over her sweatpants and her chest had barely sprouted. She wore an A-cup to make herself feel better, but really she didn't think anyone noticed when she went braless. At the moment her admiration for them plummeted; beautiful or not, they were an annoyance!

Two voices, one female the other male, argued in the breezeway, the open air hallway between the apartments, upsetting her, but also piquing her natural teenage curiosity. She peered through the peephole hoping to catch sight of someone in the breezeway between the apartments but all she saw was the apartment across the hall. Her own front door blocking the view of the adjoining apartment.

"I hate you!" Then the door slammed so hard it made the walls tremble and the door shake. Alison's face pressed against the door, she yelped from the jolt against her nose. Rubbing it, she moved away and strolled back to the kitchen, picked up her tumbler and poured filtered water into it, drinking it all in several successive gulps. Catching her breath she considered her options. She could knock on their door and ask them nicely to lower their music or she could wait it out.

Home alone, as her mother worked as a nurse at Flagler hospital, and hundreds of miles from her father and best friend, she was unsure what to do, but didn't feel knocking on the door was the best choice. Actually, the idea freaked her out. Instead, she padded to the coffee table, picked up her tablet and checked the time. She was overly dismayed when her tablet screen displayed eleven p.m.

A tad scared but nosy and irritated, she slid the patio door open and listened, maybe they were wrapping up the party. All she heard was murmuring half-drowned by the music. Upset, lonely and slightly frightened she sent her BFF in Virginia a message: *I hate my life. New neighbors are crazy. I miss you.* She knew Vicky was asleep like normal people and wouldn't see her message for several more hours.

Alison laid her phone on the table and gazed towards the heavens. A chunk of moon peeked out from the surrounding clouds. Always interested in lunar phases as most paranormal books she read featured the moon was an important piece of the story, and each phase having a specific meaning. The most well-known were the werewolves who morphed during a full moon, but red moons and blue moons had meanings too. Her body shuddered as the party next door continued, but the steady purr of a familiar vehicle kept her plastered to the chair.

Within seconds an emerald green Charger hugged the road as it passed her screened patio. Her eyes moved with it as the driver swung around the curve. She jumped from the plastic patio chair, grabbed her phone, her heart beating fast within her chest, and with a sigh, stepped inside. Almost forgetting her troublesome new neighbors. She slid the heavy glass door closed, bolting all the locks and tugging to be sure.

She raced toward the dining room window and parted the blinds, a large breezeway with philodendrons planted in the middle separated the apartments. She recognized the emerald green Dodge Charger and its driver, Rodham. To her, his chiseled body screamed for every teenage girl in a fifty mile radius to pay attention. He lived kitty corner to her apartment and directly across the hall from the new, loud neighbors.

He rounded the corner of the building, keys jingling in his hands, eyes shooting a glance across the hall towards the partying neighbors' apartment. Well defined muscles on his forearm bulged as he twisted the key in the lock. She imagined herself wrapped in those arms, his full lips kissing her neck and drifting behind her ears. Still a virgin with no prospects or past boyfriends, thoughts of Rodham filled her waking and sleeping mind. Under no circumstances did she think a hot, dreamy creature like Rodham would date an ordinary, overweight, ginger like her because she lacked the talent and looks to suck men into her web. Rodham closed the door and her moment of teenage lust ended.

Dropping the blinds, she sauntered to the fridge and lifted the papers hung on the fridge with magnets, searching for an emergency number for the apartment complex. Her mother was organized, down to every detail. As the thought brushed through her mind, she glanced at the pillows still lying on the floor and made a mental note to pick them up before bed.

With a triumphant grin, she found the number and lifted it off the fridge. Loud neighbors at eleven p.m. was an emergency in her book. She dialed the number and it directed her to leave a message. *What if I was dying? What if someone broke in and I was shivering in terror in my closet? Whatever*, she shrugged and left a message, tossed the pillows onto the couch and crawled into bed, drawing the comforter over her head, and sticking in her earbuds. She turned up the volume, attempting to drown the commotion next door and opened her tablet to her current book, *City by the Bay*.

Thirty minutes later a pounding on the front door interrupted her reading, and a shudder ran down her spine. She curled further under her covers like a frightened turtle inside its shell.

Rodham

A bottle cap skittered across the cement breezeway as Rodham rounded the corner. It landed in the dirt next to a philodendron leaf. A shattered glass bottle twinkled in the lights, its contents sprayed across the cement wall, puddling on the concrete beneath. The heavy beat from the music across the hall thumped against his eardrums.

When he drove past the apartment, he captured a glimpse of the new neighbors. Several people stood on the patio, each holding drinks in their hands. The sliding glass door open, he saw into their apartment, where a woman with blondish hair danced against a dark haired man. Her back rubbing his chest, she slid down him, her flowing hair trailing across his torso. Her partner leaned his face towards hers as she grabbed a handful of his dark hair.

Rodham fumbled with the lock, aware the apartment across the hall was empty when he'd left with his friend, Adrian, for Daytona to surf. Now, new, annoying neighbors partied and littered the breezeway. He wondered how the quiet ginger next door was faring against the noise. Always aloof with her tablet in front of her face - at the beach, the pool, slung in a hammock on the shore of the manmade lake at the apartment complex.

Her amber eyes mysterious and deep, ginger hair trailing her back with gentle waves falling across her shoulders, freckles kissed her porcelain cheeks. Intent on her tablet, she always twisted stray strands between her fingers. From the corner of his eye he caught her amber eyes peering from her parted blinds, biting her natural cherry colored bottom lip, watching as he hurried and closed the door, locking out the new, annoying neighbors.

One finger pushed against his ear, his cell phone meshed against his other, Rodham's father acknowledged he was home with a quick flash of his eyes, then he squinted and bent over talking to the person on the other end of the line.

His mom sat, feet propped on the coffee table and plugs in her ears. Her back against the soft cushion of the sectional. Closed captioning jogged across the TV screen. She waved at him as he disappeared into his room. Beach sand stuck to every part of his body, he gathered clean clothes and rushed into the shower.

He allowed the warm water to wash the sand down the drain, the cute ginger filling his thoughts. Fully focused on her, a set of dagger-tipped fangs interrupted his thoughts. A single drop of blood hung in the air as it fell from the point of a fang. A thunderous knock blasted him out of the vision. Catching the shower's side handle to keep from slipping, he knocked the back of his head against the tile wall, hard enough to give him a temporary headache. He scurried out of the shower, both his parents' were watching something through the parted blinds.

About the Author

Elle is a California native transplanted in Florida. She leads a quiet life living with her youngest daughter and granddaughter. When she's not writing she's studying the complexities of biology, streaming movies, relaxing in the sun or running off to another book signing.

www.ingramcontent.com/pod-product-compliance
Lightning Source LLC
Chambersburg PA
CBHW051646180726
48284CB00006B/1889